Journey Through the Dark Woods

Journey Through the Dark Woods

Bni Mury
To my Brother in Law
cause you are cool!

and to an awesome sister!
Bni Mury

Bonnie Murray

Copyright © 2009 by Bonnie Murray.

ISBN: Softcover   978-1-4415-2635-9

All rights reserved. No part of this book may be reproduced or transmitted in any form or by any means, electronic or mechanical, including photocopying, recording, or by any information storage and retrieval system, without permission in writing from the copyright owner.

This is a work of fiction. Names, characters, places and incidents either are the product of the author's imagination or are used fictitiously, and any resemblance to any actual persons, living or dead, events, or locales is entirely coincidental.

This book was printed in the United States of America.

To order additional copies of this book, contact:
Xlibris Corporation
1-888-795-4274
www.Xlibris.com
Orders@Xlibris.com
60666

Contents

PART 1

1: Keara 11
2: Show me the Answers... 15
3: Concerning Magick 18
4: Daligulven Strike... 23
5: Of Parting and Fighting.. 29
6: Traveling in Tents 36
7: In the Now... 42
8: Finding Herself.. 48
9: The End of Thoughts 52

PART 2

1: Fang... 59
2: Mist over Their Eyes.. 63
3: Sorting out Thoughts.. 66
4: Dreams 73
5: Green Eyes... 79
6: Returning Memories 86
7: The Plan Begins 93
8: Into the Fray.. 99
9: The Changing of a Soul 103
10: Her Suffering...110

I dedicate this book too my Caitie, for without her none of this would of happened. And for my loving Husband who has helped me too get this story out in the world. Also too my family, my mom, dad and sister Jen for always being there and helping me out in the world. I love you all!

PART 1

1

Keara

IN THIS WORLD of the mundane, I live in England, on a quite little street in a moderately priced flat, and am just about too reach the age of eighteen. My mind is always in the clouds of my writings, I work as a short story columnist in a local paper. And I also review books, and being allowed too keep all of the books I read, I have accumulated hundreds of them, all of different styles and genres. In my spare time I write my own stories and attempt too get them published on my own. So far, sadly, no one had taken any of them. My home life was not at all ordinary; I had been raised by my Grandmother for my parents had died in a robbery when I was but a baby. I don't remember them, and have no pictures of them either. But my sweet Gran had taken care of me, and she is my only family.

On one ever cloudy English morning, I emerged from my flat for a simple walk. I tried too submerge myself in too the human culture, even though the mortal world wrecked havoc on too my normally quit mind. But being a writer I knew that creativity and writing thrived on real life experiences. Staring in too one of the many antique shops that lined the roads, I grimaced at my reflection in the polished glass. I was pale, being English and not going out too much could do that too you, my waist length hair was pulled in too a loose pony tail too get it out of my face. It was a unique color; my bangs were a muted blonde, whilst the rest of it was a rich auburn. The reflection did nothing for my eyes which were normally a rich brown, but instead it had dimmed them out too black on its cold surface. My clothes were baggy and comfortable, sometimes I realized that I looked the part of a poor writer, for I hated the normal fashions of the world and tended too just dress for comfort. And normally I would just stay in my pajamas through the day, but today was different. I wanted too buy a flower . . . maybe a bouquet of them; they would look lovely in my kitchen. Keeping my eyes on the pavement under my sneakers, I finally found a new flower shop that had never caught my eye before.

The flowers that were clustered in the window were all exotic, blooms of gold and silver, intertwined with all of the colors of the rainbow. Gasping in disbelief at the veracity of all of the plants, I rushed in too the open door, and breathed deeply, for all of the scents had pervaded the air. My mind was over come with the flower shop, for its carpet was actual grass that sprang up from the ground, and saplings of various different trees were spontaneously placed around. My mouth gaped at the vision of it all,

"Ah" I whispered, as I saw a young girl standing by a group of saplings with a watering pal. Her hair was short and black with long bangs, and her clothing was modern and slimming.

"Excuse me, can you help me with something." I whispered, my voice was shy, she turned, and glared at me with cold glass blue eyes, like a husky's, I wasn't sure it they were contacts or her real eyes.

"What do I look like, a knowledgably flower girl? Phhht, you humans . . ." she grumbled and continued too water the trees around her. Taken back by her grumpy attitude, I pressed on.

"Excuse me, but you do work here, don't you?" the girl again turned too me, setting down the water can, she put a hand on her slender hip and glared at me, even though she was about the same height as me, she had a large and powerful presence about her. And automatically I felt myself shying away from her forceful glare.

"No, I don't work here, thank you very much. I am just here waiting for someone. She should be around shortly . . . well hopefully . . . See I need a replacement Earth Guardian." I tilted my head at the strange girl, but she continued too talk and glare at me. "Ya see, one of them is about to die . . . shame really, she was a good one . . . One dies, another is awaken, so I am here, finding the new replacement. I am hoping this wont take long, I have a horrible creature I need too punish a bit more." she turned away from me and continued too water the plants, my mind was reeling with the knowledge she had just said. Earth Guardians? What were those? Who was this lunatic, and who had hired her?

"Well . . . I guess I'll just be going . . ." side stepping and retracing my way out of the shop. I heard her sharp voice behind me.

"Nunda, ist sherunda, norta rha." she whispered, I stopped and listened, the language was strange, but before I could think I was replying in it as though I had known how too speak it all along. The girl was suddenly behind me and gripping my arm.

"You're the one! Good, I don't have too wait any more." she said and spun me around, blinking slowly, I stared dumbfounded at her. Was she going too take me from England, away from everything I knew? What horrible things would she do too me?

"I don't think I am, please let me go." my voice was faltering, and shaking, the girl's eyes glowed with a new ferocity, and she smiled fiercely at me.

"Oh yea you are, now come with me!" she growled to me, adrenaline ran through my body, as I shoved her away from me and rushed out of the shop. Running as fast as my legs could take me; I soon slowed and stood near a small beige flat. Leaning up against the fence that surrounded the side yard, I heard a loud growling bark behind me. Jumping I turned quickly and found a floppy eared golden retriever mix staring longingly at me with big brown eyes. Cooing lightly, I patted the dogs head and sighed,

"Jumping because of you, I guess my nerves are just on edge, eh girl?" the dog tilted its head at me from behind the fence and pranced away from me, watching the dogs wagging tail, I had a sudden sense that I was being watched.

"You do catch on quickly don't ya girlie, now how about we stop running, and you just come with me quietly." a girls voice sounded behind me, spinning around again, I noticed no one was there.

"Where are you?" I stammered out, a laugh echoed near me, too my surprise the girl in the flower shop appeared in front of me. She was different though, her skin was tinted orange, and she had a very cat like presence about her, including a long swooshing tail, and ears on the top of her head, which was now covered in an orange mane. She was also wearing a very exotic flowing costume that didn't leave too much too the imagination.

"What the . . . you're, no?" I stammered as I turned too run away from the crazy woman once more.

SMACK! My nose collided with something large in front of me, upon opening my eyes from the impact, there was nothing there, pushing my hands against the invisible force, it gave way and I feel heavily too the Earth. A curse escaped my lips, as the girl's boisterous laugh enveloped my mind.

"Oh that's just so cute! No more running girl, you get too come with me."

Following the psycho from the flower shop, whom had introduced herself as Juniper, I trailed behind her too another small house. By the house was a quant little yard that had a tent set up in the middle of it. It was just a normal blue camping tent.

"Um . . . why are we here?" I asked, Juniper laughed again and pointed too the tent.

"That is how we are getting to our destination. Get in!" opening the tent and shoving me in, I sat upon the padded bottom of the tent.

"We're traveling . . . in a tent . . . I don't understand?" I told her my mind was afraid of what would happen now that we were alone. Was she a kidnapper, stealing young girls to be sold on the black market? But that didn't explain why now she looked so feline, it made my head swirl.

"Well here are the facts. I am going too take you too the Darkwoods, there I will unlock whatever magickal abilities you have and there you will go through a trial." I attempted too voice my opinions on the trial, but Juniper pressed on. "Then you will be a full fledged Earth Guardian and you can go about doing council work and different errands." tilting my head, I watched as Juniper lay down upon the padded floor of the tent.

"I have two questions . . ." She nodded, and allowed me too continue, watching me with cold glinting eyes.

"What is the Darkwoods? And why are we in a tent?" sighing, Juniper rolled her eyes and looked back at me; I chewed on my lip nervously.

"The Darkwoods is a horrible place, it was created long ago too hold the evil that got out of hand. Demons of all varieties are cast in too there . . . most of the time by me or an Earth Guardian. It is full of dangers that will test you too see if you are cut out for this work. For you're second question, I can't teleport you directly too the Darkwoods. The first time a human teleports it normally is such a jarring experience that it disorients them for about . . . a week . . . you don't have a week in the Darkwoods. So we figured out an easier way too make you younglings travel. The idea for the tent was nice, for the new kids get too sit and rest for a bit. We will be shifting through the dimension of time and finally ending in the Immortal realm . . . now no more questions, you need too sleep!" she bellowed and curled up on too the ground. Blinking slowly, I thought through what she had told me. Darkwoods, demons, Earth Guardians? I had a thousand more questions but the girl in front of me didn't want too answer them. Why was I always in the dark? Juniper's realistic tail kept swirling and twitching, a childish impulse swept over me. I quickly reached out my hand and pulled on her tail.

"YOOOOARRRRRR . . . What the hell!!!! DON'T YOU EVER DO THAT AGAIN!" I quickly let out an apology, as she slumped back down. Grumbling and growling,

"Yea yea, I know . . . every other trainee does it . . . why would you be different . . . now PLEASE go too sleep!" she glowered as her eyes closed. Sighing too myself, I lay down and allowed my eyes too sleep. As the time drifted on, I felt the world shifting, and the weather growing colder.

2

Show me the Answers

TIME WAS MOVING in some sort of fashion, for when I awoke, it was darker outside, and cold, I shivered, and saw that Juniper was awake and opening the tent flap.

"Oh good, you're awake, I was just going too smack you too get you up but now you saved me the trouble." she grinned at me, baring sharp teeth; I sat up quickly, and followed her out. Gasping, I did a double take on the area around me. Trees that were black and gnarled stood everywhere; the earth was hard and rocky with decaying leaves covering most of it. Shadows played along the foliage; as though creatures of unknown origins watched, and waited for an opportunity too attack. No sun light shown in the sky, it was over cast and dark gray.

"Where are we?" my voice was a quiver, as I stared at the demented place.

"Oh this is the Darkwoods, I'm going too get you started on you're little . . . test. Now I need you too sit down, yea like that." I sat down, cross legged, as Juniper sat in front of me. She placed her hands against my head. They radiated heat through me; she was mumbling something in the strange language she had used earlier. A golden light seeped through her fingers and glistened across my skin, my eyes widened as things took on a new light. Everything had a pulsating color, mostly dark in this place, but I could see it, a thin fuzzy line around everything!

"Oh my . . . wow . . ." I whispered as I looked around, Juniper smiled again, and stood up swiftly.

"Now, we need too test this, point at that tree there, summon the energy around you and destroy It." obeying her, I stared at the tree then wondered how I could make it work with just pointing at it. Slowly something inside of me tugged at the energy around it, it exploded in a huge thing of sparks. It made the darkness hide away, but as soon as it diminished it crept back over us.

"Good . . . good indeed . . . okay good luck!" Juniper said and started too saunter off, my mind raced, she was leaving me? Jumping up I grabbed hold of her, she glared at me.

"I thought I told you this was you're test . . . oh wait . . . did I not explain the rules?" I shook my head, hoping she would continue. "You get three days . . . too get out of here, use you're new skills and whatever knowledge you have . . . and good luck!" before I could scream at her for more direction on this 'test' she was gone. I feel forward, and sat upon my knees, despair slowly washed over me. Sniffing back tears, I stood up, and clenched my fists tightly.

"I can do this . . ." I whispered, something near me shifted in the woods, my instincts took over and I ran. Demons, she had said, demons live in this place, how on Earth was I supposed too fight creatures like that! My legs took me far, but soon I realized I was still in a place that looked like a rotted forest. How am I going too get out? I thought too myself, as I sat down by one of the demented trees. Breathing heavily I watched the wilderness around me, nothing was out there, not that I could see anyway. Leaning my head on my knees, I sighed.

"Just great . . . I liked my quite little life . . . but no . . ." I chocked out a hoarse laugh, but soon my mind was awake again, as something crashed through the brush near me. Sitting up, I stared, as an overly large black wolf walked out of the trees. It paused and stared back at me. No wolf on Earth had ever been that big, not even an American Timber wolf, which I had only seen in pictures. The wolf tilted its head at me, but then continued on, as though it didn't pay much attention too me. Leaning back against the tree, which groaned and protested too my weight. I let out a slow breath, the creature wasn't interested in me . . . but it didn't look like a demon. Could demons take any shape they choose? So many questions were unanswered. Couldn't Juniper have given me better details on the place?

"Maybe a book?" I thought out loud.

"Who needs a books?" a voice echoed, it was definitely a male voice, with a thick accent on it; it sounded like my own actually, but with a very different dialect. Leaning farther back on the tree, I squinted in too the dark foliage around me.

"Who's there!?" I shouted, the voice laughed, I quickly stood up, and concentrated on the strange power that Juniper had shown me.

"Hey now chica, I am not gonna hurt ya. I'll come out slowly, okay?" the voice told me, he then appeared, he was taller then I and well built, he wore dark clothing with a frayed black jacket over it. Rumpled sneakers were adorned on his feet as well. His hair was shaggy and dark blonde, whilst his eyes were bright and green,

JOURNEY THROUGH THE DARK WOODS

one of them held a scar above his eyebrow, but his eyes held knowledge and fire that I had never seen before. He smiled almost a mocking smile.

"Hey, you're A LOT better lookin' then the last girl who came through here." his smile got bigger as the look of disgust grew upon my face. Just great, I find another human in this horrible world and he's a letch!

"That's not very nice, and if you're not a nice person, then I'll just get out of here myself." I quickly turned and walked away, there were no clear paths in this forest, so I just choose a direction away from the strange man.

"Hey, don't be angry! I don't get many visitors who are mostly human. I'm sorry I swear it!" he called, as he ran up and caught hold of my arm. Quickly I turned around and hit my knee forward, striking him between the legs. That is what happens when you live alone, you get good reflects, and don't think about what might happen. He quickly doubled over and let out many curses, but again looked up at me.

"Okay . . . I deserved that . . . ouch, wow girl you're pretty strong for such a little thing." he said, as he got back up. I glared at him, he seemed like he had meant the apology earlier, but I still didn't know if I could trust this odd fellow with my life in a place like this.

"Stop calling me girl . . . or chica! I have a name, its Keara." I said, crossing my arms in front of me. He smiled, and stretched up a little bit, showing me that physically, he was much bigger then me.

"Nice too know, I'm Fang, if you would like the help, I can get you out of here, and in you're little three day limit." his smile broadened, as amazement danced over my features. This random man, whom called himself Fang, could help me get out of here? He knew of the three day limit. Maybe he could also help me actually get home and away from this cursed place!

3

Concerning Magick

WALKING WITH FANG, taught me a couple of things one was. Never judge a book by its cover, and two was, how uninteresting a mortal life can be after being trapped here for a long time.

"What do you mean; you've been here a 'long time' like ten years? You can't be much over twenty five." I asked him as we walked through the never ending trees.

"Well . . . it's sort of a long story, but I was put here about . . . three hundred years ago?" he scratched his head, and shrugged, staring at him, my jaw went slack, he tilted an eyebrow at me.

"What?" he asked, looking confused.

"You're three hundred years old?" I asked stupidly, his eyebrow remained in the same place, but after a second, he started laughing. I took the offensive and crossed my arms at him.

"Actually chica . . . I'm a little over a thousand years old." my mouth fell open again, and his boisterous laughter filled the dark place we were amerced in. Finally getting over the fact that I was walking with someone who had been born in the dark ages (if my math and history was right, Fang would have been born after the time of King Arthur . . . if you believed in him that is). We continued our walk which turned out too be not that stimulating of an experience, for the black trees were the only things I could see in this haunting place.

JOURNEY THROUGH THE DARK WOODS

"So . . . if you're an immortal, does that mean I am too?" I asked my face reddened with the look he gave me, as though I was a child. Well too him I was, but I pressed on that he answer.

"Any mortal who comes here is automatically an immortal yes, if you're a Were Creature of some sort, you age at a set limit, a year for every hundred of so. But if you are say, well an Earth Guardian, you don't age, at all." he smiled, as though his knowledge should impress me. I decided too push on with more topics.

"Do you know anything about magick? And why earlier did you call me mostly human, I am human still, right?" I asked him, he shrugged, he didn't seem like he wanted too answer, which made me a little irritated, I wanted too know what had happened too me. Quickly I told him about making the tree explode, he smiled ruefully at me.

"Well that makes sense; Earth Guardians use energy magicks and Earth magicks. You were just drawing on the energy around you, too create another destructive energy. Don't worry once you get out of here, you can find a teacher for all of this or just read a lot. And I have no idea if Earth Guardians are considered human, you would have too ask another one . . . I think you still are?" his answer didn't sit well with me but I decided not too pester him about it more if he couldn't tell me. Asking him if there were any other sorts of magicks, he told in not so much detail that there is one other. A sort of dark magick, blood and ritual types that were against the Earth Guardians laws.

"You don't want too get mixed up in that stuff Luv, its bad news." he shuddered a little bit. Dropping the topic again I continued walking, after a while Fang asked me some questions.

"So . . . you're from England right?" I nodded, he grinned, and set a slightly faster pace, I had too almost jog too keep up with him. For his legs were a lot longer then my own, it wasn't my fault I was short, even my grandmother was a bit taller then I and last I checked I was only about five three. I was about too ask him what his question meant when he stopped dead in his tracks and stared off in too the encroaching darkness. I hadn't noticed but with what little light we were getting that it was vanishing in too the darkness.

"What's wrong?" I asked, he didn't respond, a low growl filled his throat, he sounded like a great animal I stepped away from him. And looked where he was staring, something was moving about in the darkness near us. It had very little form, but I could make out pale sickly flesh and glowing red eyes.

"What is it?" I asked softly, soon it vanished; Fang slumped his shoulders, and looked relieved.

"It was a lesser demon, nasty little buggers, but they normally don't mess with me. So we're safe." he said and patted me on the head, I glared at him for again treating me like a child, but didn't voice it. He probably didn't think much of me, just a thing too pass the time of being here forever.

"Why won't the demons bother us?" I asked, as we continued too walk. It seemed like we would probably be walking most of this trip. It bothered me that I only knew of one form of aggressive magick and nothing that would be defensive. I sighed and waited for his answer.

"Well . . . I've lived here for a long time . . . and well, they just know not too mess with me . . . So . . . in England . . . what is it like now?" he quickly had the topic changed, and I didn't push it, if it came too a pushing match I think he would of won.

"Its okay, over cast days most of the time, lots of rain, I work as a writer, and live in a nice flat by a little park. And I try to visit my Grandmother as much as I can; she is in a nursing home because of her lungs. But besides that it is alright."

"What about you're parents? Are they going too be worried about you?" he asked, his eyes full of wonder, I stared back at him wondering what was going through his mind, then I finally answered. I didn't quite understand why I was rattling on with my answers; I guess I was just nervous.

"I don't remember my parents, my Grandmother raised me . . . she's such a nice lady, her name is Ehlorra. I think it's a pretty name, she told me that I was named after my mother, when I was only about two weeks old they were killed by armed robbers . . . they shot them. That's what I'm told anyway . . . what about you . . . what are you're parents like?" I quickly wanted too change how I said that, Fang was old, his parents were probably dead as well, when he answered dead, I simply nodded my head, he didn't say anymore.

"Ehlorra . . . sounds familiar, but I guess it could be a popular name. See about eighty or so years ago, a nice new Earth Guardian came through, I think that was her name. She was also from England, I guess she's dead, seeing as you're here." he said, no emotion was in his voice, as he looked on too the ever growing night. Another woman by that name? And she had been an Earth Guardian? An odd thought, but I didn't have much time too think about it. We walked near a large canopy of trees, twisted and gnarled; they had formed a crude structure, almost like a house.

"Oh can we sleep there tonight?" I asked walking towards the place, putting a strong arm out, Fang stopped me from going near it.

"No, that's a bad place, a witch was cast in too here, for using blood magick, and she lived there. She was finally killed by a demon she tried too summon. Many creatures have put curses upon that place . . . there's a place where we can stay up ahead." he said, his voice was low and raspy as he had recited it too me. Looking away, we continued on our relentless trek. Finally, I saw another tiny structure in the distance. When inquiring what it was Fang told me it was a rest stop.

"They have rest stops here?" I asked he laughed and patted me on the back; I was getting a little annoyed with how much physical touch he used on me. For I knew we weren't close enough too warrant any, but he didn't seem too notice and shortly he quickened our pace yet again.

JOURNEY THROUGH THE DARK WOODS

"Yea, they were set up before I got here. There's about four of them in this place. All about the same though." seeing the structure up close, I noticed that the twisted trees formed a sort of barrier around the place, and made it look like a normal porch, like one on a house. There were small pallets filled with straw in the center of it.

"It looks sort of . . . used?" I whispered, Fang laughed again and sat down on the edge of it. I sat down besides him. Watching as the light faded from the world, a sense of wonder took control, small lights danced about the dying trees. Sighing, I pushed my bangs out of my face and smiled too myself.

"Why are you so happy?" Fang asked his voice uncertain, he had an odd look upon his face, and I wasn't a people person, so I couldn't read it.

"It's just . . . its sort of beautiful here . . . in a different sort of way . . . do any of the girls you help out ever stay?" Fang's eyes wandered around the area we were in, letting out a yawn, he shook his head.

"Nah, they don't . . . they don't like it here . . . they are afraid . . . they fear me and everything near me, they always run as soon as I show them the border." Looking away, his shaggy hair swept over his eyes, as he stared off. Looking back at the little lights, I felt sorry for Fang, he seemed nice enough, even though his ego was a bit big. Why would these girls be afraid of him? And what had he done?

"Um . . . Fang . . . may I ask you a personal question?" He nodded, and allowed me too voice my question. "What did you do too get stuck here?" I asked in a small voice, he looked back, and shook his head, making his hair flip out of his face.

"That is a good question. I did bad stuff, stuff I would never do again . . . things that I want to forget about . . . but I'm different. It was Juniper who finally found me, tortured me and threw me in here. And here I have been sense." his voice was low, I could barely make it out, I watched as his eyes darkened with the memories. Chewing on my bottom lip, I didn't press it. Did I want too know what he had done? My curiosity did, but I couldn't ask him, he seemed too deep in thought or might get offended that I ask that personal of a question, especially sense we didn't know each other that well.

"Any more questions for the night Chica cause you should sleep." he finally said, as he stared in too the night sky, where stars were starting too wink down on us.

"What do you know of the Earth Guardians . . . sadly Juniper doesn't like telling people anything." switching the topic seemed too make Fang a bit happier, he let out a low chuckle and shook his head again, allowing his hair too fly around.

"I don't know much, but I'll tell ya what I know. They have been around for a long time, they are older then I am. After Were Creatures and Vampires were created . . . by God knows who, humans slowly became magick users, by means we don't know. Finally the magick users banded together and created the Earth Guardians, too protect the Earth from the things in the Immortal Realm . . . Um . . . lets see . . . they are all women, Juniper is the main leader . . . and they use magick . . . there are two in each continent . . . that's all I can think of. I don't know much about magick users . . . sorry bit." scratching his head, he sent a sideways glance at me, I smiled at him.

"You're way too happy on being here . . . you're an odd one." chuckling he stood up on the porch, giving him a defiant look; I tried too sound as menacing as I could.

"Well if you're so normal, you wouldn't be here, so I guess maybe I am not normal . . . which" – I paused as I thought on this, my voice became lighter – "is different, I always knew I wasn't connected too the people in my world. They were all so strange too me. I guess I have finally found my place too be." blowing out my cheeks, I kicked the edge of the porch lightly with my feet.

"Yea, you're weird . . . but I am glad you're here. It gets a bit lonely . . ." Fang let his voice drift off, as he lent me a hand too get up on the porch more easily. Seeing as it had no steps. I thanked him, as I sat down on one of the lumpy make shift mattress.

"Well it could be worse I guess . . . we could be on the ground." I whispered, Fang nodded and sat down on the opposite one, laying down I stared up in too the sky again. A cold breeze swished by me, sending a shiver through me. Fang noticed, and quickly took off his jacket and handed it too me.

"I'll be fine, just a bit cold." I told him, throwing the jacket on top of me; he gave me a stern look, like a father telling off a naughty child.

"It gets a lot colder the darker it gets. So take it, I'll be fine, I'm a warm blooded sort of guy." he smiled, an almost reassuring look, again I thanked him and wrapped it around me. A musky sweet smell emanated from it, it was almost a pleasant sort of scent, making my mind fog over and allowing sleep too over take me.

4

Daligulven Strike

SO MANY THINGS raced through my head, images, and thoughts that were not my own, nor did I ever remember doing them. It felt as though it was not my body being moved about. I was in a dark place, someone was with me, and I couldn't see them, though being with them meant I was safe, and nothing in the world could hurt me. Then why, with this feeling, was I in so much pain. Tears were running down my face, I wanted too scream for it to be over, for this person to help me . . .

With a jolt, I awoke too the smell of fire and meat, I quickly sat up, and looked around me. Light had returned too the Darkwoods, the magick I had felt earlier had ceased. Wondering where the smell was coming from I looked over too the edge of the porch. Fang was crouched in front of a small campfire that he must have made up, he was holding a stick, and upon that stick there was a chunk of meat on it. His eyes had never left the fire, he stared in too it, making the green in his eyes fade too a menacing blaze. Tilting my head, I wondered what he was thinking, with that feral look on his face. Suddenly he looked up, his eyes going back too their normal brightness.

"Finally you're awake. I thought you'd sleep all day. Hungry?" he asked, as he held up the stick, I quickly got up from the mat and unwrapped myself from his jacket. Standing up, he leaped up on too the deck with ease and handed me the stick, which I took and exchanged his coat for. Raising an eyebrow at it, I sniffed it, it smelled edible enough. And soon I found myself taking large bites of it. I had forgotten that I hadn't eaten sense breakfast the day before.

"This is really good, what is it?" I asked, as Fang sat across from me, eyeing the food I was consuming, I offered him whatever was left. His laughter bubbled up again.

"Nah, I already ate, it's actually deer I found the bugger near here. Stupid things make their way in too the Darkwoods all the time." he said, as he was talking, I noticed that there was fresh blood upon the shirt that he had been wearing the night before. Not saying anything, I allowed my mind too tell itself that it was from the deer. Something inside of me was making me worry, but with Fang's bright attitude for the day, I quickly shoved it away.

After I was done eating, we headed back through the demented trees that seemed to go on forever. Brushing my hair back and re-doing my ponytail, I wondered how Fang handled being here for so long. It must get lonely, as he had said, and for three hundred years, what did one do. Many more questions ran through my mind as the day wore on. Soon Fang's voice brought me too the present.

"So . . . I have too know something, when you first met Juniper did she appear in a flower shop?" his question caught me off guard but I answered it with a yes.

"Ah . . . well . . . did you buy a flower?"

"What would that have to do with anything?" I asked him, his eyes had grown concerned, and I wondered if this had another secret meaning, I voiced this concern.

"If you buy a flower from Juniper she can trace you through the Darkwoods, see what you are seeing . . . I was just wondering, because . . . well . . . she sort of hates me. And I didn't want too get you in too trouble with her." he ran a hand through his hair, and watched me for a response.

"Oh . . . dear . . . well good thing I didn't. She sort of scared me actually . . . so I ran off, but no, I am not linked too her . . . I guess." the thought made me shiver; too have Juniper watching in on me, it made my stomach knot. As the walk continued we came too a part of the forest that was so thick we had to slow down so our clothing didn't get caught on the branches. The foliage seemed as though they were trying too strangle us, Fang had an easier time then myself, though he was bulkier then I, he was a lot stronger. Taking hold of my hand at one point he pulled me through the thicket, tripping over my own feet, I started too fall over; luckily Fang's large frame caught me. I was a slightly clumsy person, but never before had someone caught me; I pulled back from him and found myself blushing. A small tinge of red had also spread through Fang's face. I didn't ask him if he was embarrassed or not, all I did was thank him, and continue.

Before we got too far, something came through the brush at an astonishing speed. The creatures leapt from the surrounding woods, I felt myself gasp, as one of the creatures knocked over Fang who didn't have time too react. Growling, Fang pushed the creature off of himself. Upon further notice, they were large wolves. Not like the one I had seen earlier, that was all black, instead they were muted red, and grays, all of them looked large and powerful. Fang jumped back on too his feet, his eyes flashing a feral look at the wolves.

"Talon." he spat, the creature, Talon, whom had knocked him over just made a garbled laughing noise, it sent shivers through me. I felt the energy that Juniper had shown me rise around me, the others felt it as well.

"Grab the witch!" the leader snarled, as the other two creatures sat up right and grabbed hold of my arms, they had vise like grips, their paws were more like hands with elongated claws and digits. Fang's eyes never had left the leaders. I tried to shake them away from me, but their grips never faltered, they watched their leader as well.

"Leave her alone Talon, this is not you're territory, we can pass through!" he said, his voice had dropped low, and also sounded like a growl. The leader howled in laughter.

"Everywhere you go will be the Daligulven's territory, you horrible excuse of an Aukoc!" his voice was such a gravely growl, I could barely understand him, I tried too break free of the wolves that held me, but my strength couldn't do anything against them. They all laughed with their foul smelling breath of blood and decay, which made me gag.

"Leave Talon . . . You don't want too fight me!" Fang's voice grew louder, with my new found eye sight, I saw that the small light that surrounded him started too increase and swirl. Magick? No it didn't feel like magick, and Fang had said he didn't know magick, it was something else, something that felt like raw primitive power.

"Oh come now, Silver Fang, don't you want too join us again, and maybe have a little fun with this girl, she's probably a screamer isn't she Fang? Just like the old days!" Talon's voice got louder as well, the energy around Fang exploded.

"TAKE THAT BACK YOU BASTARD!" he yelled and leapt at the creature, I called his name in fear how could he fight such a creature? As he leapt, his body lurched and twitched, as a wolf's form erupted from his physic. Black and sleek, he was much larger then the leader and his eyes were a more intense yellow. Showing large teeth, he tackled the leader. They feel to the ground, thrashing and snapping. My mind swirled with what was before me . . . Fang, was a giant wolf? A moment of recollection took me, the wolf from when I first got here? Was that him? A horrible howl brought me back too reality, Talon had Fang pinned below him, his pink jaws had clamped down on Fang's forearm.

"NO! DON'T HURT HIM!" I yelled, the golden energy filled me, the creatures holding me soon let go, yelping in fear. Both of the large wolves looked at me. Talon with blood on his face, drooling with pride, and Fang, a look of wonder on his animal face. The magick surged though me, sending the ball of energy at Talon it struck him in the face, making him back away from Fang, his fur singed and skin blistering. Howling in despair, the other wolves tried too make it too their wounded leader, Fang was faster, he lurched forward, grabbing Talon's throat in his massive jaws he threw the fallen leader too the ground. Releasing him, Fang lunged at Talon's chest, and bit through the bones and sinew protecting the inner workings of his torso. I feel too my knees, the energy was leaving my limbs, I was useless. Looking back up, Fang's head jerked up, something bloody was in his mouth, and within his powerful jaws he bit down and swallowed. Talon was dead, and the other two wolves fled. My world swam, what had just happened? Was that real, looking over, I saw Fang slowly backing away and collapsing upon the ground.

"Oh God, Fang!" I yelled, as weary as my body was my mind pushed my muscles in too working and I crawled over too him. The open wounds upon his body had stopped bleeding; new flesh was slowly forming over the bite marks. Rolling his eyes at me, in his wolf form he winked, and slowly, the wolf disappeared, and Fang laid there, his clothes were bloody and torn, but his wounds were almost done healing.

"That Talon . . . he has always been a nasty one . . ." he whispered, as he gazed up at me, a slow grin falling over his face.

"Are you alright?" I asked, wiping some of the blood off of his face with my own shirt.

"I will be . . . I'm sorry that I lied to you chica . . . I didn't want you to be afraid of Me." he grumbled as he looked away from me, slowly he sat up, I helped him the best I could.

"So . . . what are you exactly . . . Talon called you an Aukoc . . . but I don't know what that is?" I asked him, his breathing grew steadier as he sat, glancing at me, he sighed heavily.

"It's a tribe of werewolf, that's what I am, an Aukoc werewolf . . ." he whispered, as he spat out blood . . . blood? He had eaten the heart of another werewolf, my stomach knotted, I didn't allow it too get too me too much. For all I knew that could be normal.

"How did you heal like that?" I asked before my mind could question anything else.

"It's a talent that both Were's and Earth Guardians have . . . its sort of nifty . . ."

I nodded my head, his gaze hardened as he stared at me.

"You're not running in fear yet? Did I not scare you enough?" his voice was hoarse as he said this, he stood up, and stared down at me. Standing as well, I brushed my hands over my pants, and gave him a hard look.

"No . . . I am not afraid of you. You have been very kind too me. You are showing me through a god forsaken place, and you protected me. Why would I be afraid of you?"

Fang's expression almost startled me; it went from shameful to timid to joy.

"That is an interesting thought . . . someone not afraid of me . . ." before Fang could finish his thought, a line from Hamlet popped in too my head.

"There are more things in heaven and earth, Horatio, than are dreamt of in your philosophy." I said, speaking the line to the best of my knowledge, tilting his head at me, Fang looked puzzled.

"My name isn't Horatio." he said with a confused expression on his face, in this tense moment I felt laughter bubbling through me, allowing my mirth too show, I doubled over laughing. Falling down too the dirt, on my knees again, I laughed until my sides hurt, after a while, Fang helped me up from my aching crouch. He didn't ask why I had laughed so hard he was still trying to figure out the reason for me saying such odd things.

"It's from a play, by a very famous English writer, its called Hamlet . . . but that's alright . . . should we continue on our way?" I asked, he agreed, and we started again on our way, feeling better about our growing friendship. My inquiry continued.

"What's it like too be a werewolf?" I asked stupidly, he shrugged and scratched his head.

"I've been a werewolf for a thousand years luv . . . I don't really know, its weird, it's like I have two personalities. Over all, it's fine, though I hate the full moons. We loose our minds and go crazy and can't remember what we have done. It's a ruddy hell sometimes as well." he whispered, I felt an odd pang of guilt; I had no idea of what he was talking about. I had never had odd feelings like that, or went crazy. I feel silent and looked down at my feet, his voice echoed in my head.

"That's why I was actually thrown in here . . . I had killed so many . . . but not even on the full moon, I was obsessed. So here I am, helping out girls in my spare time, even though I am a demon, and most of them run screaming . . . but you didn't . . . and for that, I thank you." his voice was a hushed whisper, I lifted my eyes up too meet his but he was also looking down.

"I wont be afraid of you Fang . . . You're a nice guy, and like I said before, very helpful. You're the only friend I've ever truly had." a small laugh escaped his mouth.

"An Earth Guardian . . . friends with an Aukoc, this could be interesting." he said.

And as I found out it was very interesting indeed.

Finally, we made it too another rest stop, it was the same, but there were no mats filled with straw, just blankets all over the twisted limbs making up the deck. Plopping down on the blankets, I pulled one over myself, shivering from the growing chill in the air. Fang was silent, as he stared off at the sky; the stars had come back out.

"Hey, Fang, the constellations, I don't see any I know." I whispered, sighing, he scooted closer too me and pointed at the sky above us.

"Well, I don't know the true names, I have just made up a couple." he told me, I listened kindly, as he pointed out a couple. "That's the knowing tiger in the west, and the grinning wolf in the north . . . over there in the East that's . . . Ruby." his voice grew sad with the name, I raised an eyebrow at him but he didn't continue, laying there within the confines of this world. I realized that my world would not be the same when I returned.

My mind wandered to what my Grandma was doing, was she alright, that sudden realization came through me. I stiffened, Fang noticed, he questioned my reaction.

"I am just concerned . . . I left my Grandma all alone . . . I hope she is alright." My mind was drifting too sleep as I whispered it. Fang nodded slowly, a couple more questions needed too be asked before I could fall asleep though.

"So . . . I take it you're real name isn't Fang. What is it?" he snorted and gave me a funny look.

"It was Cody . . . but just call me Fang still, it's what most call me now . . ." I nodded slowly, and then the last coherent thought left my lips.

"You asked me if I was afraid . . . what are you afraid of?" I asked him my voice groggy with sleep weighing down upon me. I had already closed my eyes but his voice was very low and hushed.

"I am afraid of hurting people I care for . . . and loosing what is important . . . what are you afraid of?" he asked, I rolled over and sighed heavily.

"Guns . . . they are so horrible." I heard Fang say something else, I couldn't ask him to repeat it, my mind had already fallen too dreams.

5

Of Parting and Fighting

THE DEMON STOOD before me, growling, snarling, glowing red eyes, I screamed!

"Keara? Are you alright?" a voice asked me, as I woke up with a jolt, tears were streaming down my face, as I stared up in too Fang's worried eyes. I had never had nightmares before coming too this place, had something awakening inside of me. Something that I couldn't control, I pushed the thought away and tried too answer Fang.

"Yea . . . I think so?" I whispered, as I panted and lay back down, I was covered in sweat, what was this place doing too me? Sitting back Fang stared at me, puzzled as always, he tilted his shaggy head at me.

"What happened?" he asked, I quickly, told him the little bit of the dream that I remembered, and he listened patiently, as my fears spilled forth in my voice. The wind was cold against my face, as I looked away from his concerned eyes. Why was he worried, he didn't really know me that well. Did werewolves have feelings like a human, a sense too protect one's friends? I looked around the area, the little bit of light was returning. He sat patiently in front of me, his eyes also wandering. Sighing, I stood up, and stepped off of the porch.

"I think we should get out of here . . ." I whispered, he nodded and stood up a slight look of sadness played upon his features. As we continued too walk through this world of darkness, I realized that it was getting lighter, the world

29

was changing. The horrible trees were becoming sparse, and spots of green grass were randomly growing.

"Could you come with me . . . when I leave?" I asked, breaking the silence between us. Shifting his weight as he walked, he made us veer through the growing path before us.

"I'll go back here, this is where I have too stay Keara . . . forever, or until this curse is lifted." he spoke slowly, as though he was measuring his words. He had actually used my name this morning, I wondered if he was finally done with the silly nicknames, or if it held more meaning.

"What would it take too get you out of here?" I asked I felt saddened at the thought of leaving him. He was indeed my only friend, in this world and the mortal world. A light blush crept over his face, as he ran a nervous hand through his hair.

"Well . . . um . . . I have too find true love." he blurted it out, the blush crept farther on his cheeks, a blush tinted my face as well.

"Are all curses like that?" I asked he shook his head.

"No, some curses can't be broken. But mine wont get broken, the only girls who come through here are Trainee Earth Guardians, and you're so far the only girl who hasn't run from me." the blush went away from his face, as we got closer too the border. One more question puzzled my mind as we walked towards the place that held my path home.

"You and Juniper have both talked about these two worlds . . . why hasn't anyone figured out that these two places are connected?" I asked him, Fang scuffed his feet on the ground, and chewed on his lip. Measuring his words he told me.

"The Immortal realm and the Mortal realm, we know it as Earth, are very close together by dimensional stand points . . . its hard too explain. But they can only be accessed by people with a strong sense of magick. That's all I know . . ." his voice trailed off, I shrugged it off and figured I would ask someone someday about it. Maybe they could explain it too me better. The darkness in the area was soon almost washed away as we found the border.

The place was lined in dark twisted trees but there was an opening about four feet wide, I stared hard at it. On the other side was bright green grass and trees that were the most beautiful shade of emerald I had ever seen.

"Oh my, this is so lovely." I whispered, as I stared at the entrance.

"Well, it's been nice I guess . . . good luck." he whispered; as he turned around suddenly, and started too walk away. Out of impulse, I grabbed his arm. He turned back too me, sadness on his face, I felt the same sadness creep through me. I wanted him too come with me, but how could I? I didn't know how too break curses!

"Can you please try . . . please?" I whispered, he sighed and agreed, looking back, he ran towards the entrance, a course of blue lightning erupted around him. Howling in frustration and pain, he feel back, he laid there gasping with his eyes wavering.

"Are you alright?" I asked him, as he slowly got back up.

"Yea I'm fine; see I can't get out of here." A sudden though ripped through my skull. I grabbed his hand, and had him follow me through the entrance, the lightning pulsed through us both, I felt the golden energy that lay within my body rush through me and surround Fang as well. I felt a tug as I passed through the portal, using all of my strength I tugged on Fang's arm. He came through the entrance, tumbling over. We laid there laughing, he hugged me hard and we continued too laugh. His eyes were tear rimmed, as he helped me up, he was laughing so hard still, he hugged me again, then picked me up and twirled me around. Holding me, he stopped and we stood there, I was face too face with him, after a second, a blush coursed through us both as he let me down.

"Thank you, if it hadn't been for you, I would still be in that hell hole." he said, as he gave me another light hug.

"You're welcome, well I couldn't just leave you there . . . you're my friend after all." his grin became larger, and soon I was smiling as well. After a second I looked around at where we were. The large field stretched about a mile, and in the distance stood a small town . . . or a village, I couldn't tell from this distance.

"Where are we?" I asked, Fang looked around, and rubbed his chin. Which had a light stubble on it, I guess werewolves needed too shave occasionally as well.

"Well it looks like we are near Sharn . . . it's a nice little village, I went through there about four hundred years ago or so. And we should be able too get back too the mortal realm that way." we started too walk again, but this time in the sun and through a grassy field. I felt my spirits lift; I could tell that Fang was ecstatic about being out for his feet were light on the grass we walked on. But soon I had more questions.

"How are we going to get back? I don't know how too use spells like that?" I asked him, pondering this, he smiled at me.

"We'll rent a tent, like how you got here; a lot of people use them. And it takes fairly simple magick, I couldn't do it, but really, I think you could." he reassured me, as we slowly made our way too the town before us.

Tiny and tranquil it much reminded me of the villages in England that you could pass through in the country side. Many different people walked about, some humans, some cat people, some looked Elvin and there were some I had no names for. Upon entering the quite village, we soon discovered that a couple of people were watching us closely, and glaring at us. My cheeks were burning as we passed tiny homes, not much different from the houses in my world; they were all different colors and shapes. Children chased each other through the alley ways of the different homes, while motherly women gardened and watched the young ones romp about. It all seemed so unreal, as though we were disturbing it.

"Hey Fang, do you think we can get anything too eat." I hadn't eaten sense Fang had gotten that deer . . . which now that I knew he was a werewolf; I wondered how he had killed it. Licking his lips, he stared off for a second.

"Yea, I know a great place just up ahead!" he said, and hurried our pace, the people soon seemed too ignore us, so my shyness sank away. Reaching a larger building with a loaf of bread on a sign, we entered and all eyes turned too us. I felt my shyness emerge too the surface again. Every creature in there, except for a sparse group of humans, were all the same sort of cat person that Juniper was (which Fang had told me had no name for their species, because their race was so old). But in different varieties, spots, stripes and some even tabby or ginger, all looked upon us. Taking my hand, Fang led me too a table in the back where we sat down. He didn't seem to notice the glares or was ignoring them.

"So, what would you like too eat?" he asked, as we looked at a menu, Fang stared blankly at it.

"What looks good to you?" I asked him, I was very happy that the menu was in English, so I could read it. Tilting his head a little, Fang sank back on his chair, and turned his head away.

"I cant read luv . . ." he whispered, I gawked at him for a second, then the memories came back too me, he was born in the dark ages, no one knew how too read then and he had been trapped in the Darkwoods for three hundred years. I felt bad for him, but realized it wasn't his fault, I started too read him the menu, when a young girl walked up too our table. She had the same tiger like appearance as Juniper, but actually had black stripes running up and down her arms and legs, which weren't very covered, for she only wore something like a sports bra and running shorts that were a brilliant blue. Her hair was black and spiked, she smiled at us both.

"Hello, my name is Sapphire, I am one of the guards here, might I ask you, who you are and where you are traveling?" her voice was so sweet sounding, I almost replied, but Fang cut me off.

"Well you see my girl and I are just passing through, no trouble and all. We'll be out of you're hair once we leave." I felt myself blushing, he called me his girl? Was it a rouse so that Sapphire would turn a blind eye too us. I felt my heart beating faster, Fang shot me an odd look. Slamming her fists down on the table, the girl snarled at us.

"I know who and what you are Aukoc! So unless you want me too dismantle this building too take you down, I suggest we take this outside!" smirking at Sapphire, Fang slowly got up and followed her out, while he followed her he shot me a glance, giving me the stay-here-and-everything-will-be-okay look. Allowing them too exit the building I quickly got up and followed after them. Fang was my friend and I wasn't going too allow him too fight alone.

Exiting the bustling restaurant, I saw a group of people standing around what I thought would be Sapphire and Fang. Trying to make my way through the throbbing crowd was harder then I thought. After some failed attempts too get through, a rush of magick shifted through the air making my mouth dry. The air around me exploded with energy, as two huge beasts emerged from the sky. One was a black dragon creature with a daunting Tigers head, it roared in triumph and headed in too the clearing. The other creature looked like a wolf that had rust, white and black markings all over its body, with huge falcon wings. It also landed within the clearing. Fang was out numbered; I was sure those creatures were helpers of Sapphire's. Using whatever energy was left in the air, I concentrated upon getting through the crowd, and soon I shoved through. Sapphire was standing above Fang, whose arms were being held down by the giant creatures. Yelling in fear, I rushed forward, not thinking of anything else, I shoved my shoulder in too Sapphire, her smaller frame gave way and we tumbled away from Fang. The dragon tiger stepped forward, its dank breath upon my face. His growl vibrated through my bones, wincing I closed my eyes hoping that it wouldn't eat me, I heard Fang's bloodied voice behind us.

"Sueru! You can't hurt her, she's a human!" – He paused and coughed – "She is not in this fight! Leave her alone!" his voice was defiant, my eyes snapped open, the creature looked too its Master with an odd expression upon its cat features. Sapphire got up, and snarled at me, her tail was bristled with anger.

"What the hell do you think you're doing human!" she spat at me, I stood up, ignoring the imposing creatures before me, I looked at Fang, and at the wolf who was still holding his arms down. Fang's face was bloody and his shirt was torn, showing that there was a large bite in his side that was exposing ribs, with a large pool of blood already forming. My fury turned too Sapphire, I felt the energy around me growing and writhing, just asking for me too use it.

"You need too leave him alone, he's my friend." I shouted, my voice had more confidence then I had ever had in my life.

"You're an Earth Guardian?" Sapphire said, her eyes widened, she bowed too me slowly.

"Forgive me, I didn't know . . . but why do you travel with this Aukoc? He is a villain!" her voice was stern; the wolf creature looked too Sapphire and said in a low voice that sounded like water falling over stones.

"He has a soul . . . she must be his protector." his voice also held kindness in it which made me turn my head too him, his brown eyes were full of knowledge; he smiled at me and stepped off of Fang. Sapphire grumbled.

"He is right . . . I am sorry . . . but please, take him away from here, these people don't trust Werewolves." she turned away from me, her creatures returned too her side. Before she exited the dispersing crowd, the dragon looked back at me.

"Be weary of him when the full moon rises . . ." he said, and they left, I rushed too Fang, who was sitting up slowly. The blood was still welling up from his wound.

"Oh God Fang, what did they do too you?" I asked, as I inspected the wounds, he had a large gash upon his forehead, and the bite wound wasn't healing. His eyes were weary as he looked at me.

"Shouldn't these be healing?" I asked him, looking down he shrugged, and grimaced in pain.

"I guess they hold some magick . . . you'll need to do it Bit. Get rid of the magick or I think . . . wow its dark isn't it?" he asked, I looked around, the sun was still high in the sky. I put my hand over his wound, focusing on the magick around me. My eyes were starting too tear, I couldn't loose him he was my friend, and had done so much for me. I could help him, I knew I could.

"Please . . . work . . . take it out of his blood." as though the energy understood me, I felt a drain of power from my arms, as Fang coughed, and feel backwards again, lying there. His eyes rolled, the wound glowed faintly, and slowly it started too heal.

"Erf . . . that sucked . . ." he whispered, a nervous laugh escaped my lips, fear gripped my stomach, he had almost been hurt beyond repair, after a little bit, he sat back up, and shook his head. Smiling he put an arm around me.

"What would I do without you, hmm?" he asked, I chewed on my lip.

"If it wasn't for me you wouldn't be getting hurt all the time." my voice was small, he shook his head.

"Nah, I needed you, you got me out of a place that probably would of killed me . . . this was nothing." he gestured to the hole in his shirt that was now covered in his blood, his voice was very reassuring. But still the fear was eating at me, I knew he could handle fighting but I seemed too keep getting him in trouble. Luckily my only friend seemed too be good at escaping death.

"How did you know that creature's name?" I asked him, as he gazed at the sun in the sky, his face was still ashen as he looked back at me.

"Everyone knows Sueru and Black, they are Sapphire's helpers, Juniper mentioned them a couple of times, she is Juniper's cousin after all." I felt myself gasp as Fang laughed lightly at me, but still winced in pain at the movement of his chest. I allowed him too sit and rest until he was ready too move away from this place.

Finally, Fang was ready too stand, we made our way too the out skirts of the village, I found that my stomach was grumbling. As though Fang was reading my mind, or just hearing my stomach, he pointed out a tavern that was near us. A large sign hung in front of the door, "The Slaughtered Lamb" it read, I grumbled about the name, but we still entered the dark hole in the wall pub.

Sitting down at a small table in the back, a man who looked of Russian decent came too our table, his hair was a silvery blonde and his eyes were that of a wolf's.

"What shall it be?" he asked and smiled at us, with slightly pointed teeth, I frowned and looked at Fang.

"Well, how about two house special, and honey mead . . . what do you want too drink luv?" he asked me, I shrugged and asked for Pepsi.

"Ha ha, we don't serve that here dear, try the human world." The man told me, I grumbled and simply said water. Turning away he left us.

"What are house specials?" I asked, he informed me that normally it was a stew or meat of some sort, I didn't argue. I was too hungry. In my normal life, I wasn't much of a meat eater, but I didn't tell that too Fang.

JOURNEY THROUGH THE DARK WOODS

"Can you eat other things . . . besides meat?" I asked, I felt foolish, for the look he gave me, he laughed a little.

"Yea, I can eat just about anything actually. Us Aukoc's we got iron stomachs." he said, and patted his stomach and groaned slightly, I guessed the pain from his injuries still were with him. Soon the man came back, he had a plate with cheese and breads on it, and a mug of water and of mead. Fang was studying the man in an odd fashion.

"Hey, you're Manifesto, aren't you? A Faolon, right?" he asked, and raised an eyebrow, the man nodded, and introduced himself as Manifesto.

"And you must be Silver Fang, the Aukoc; I thought you were in the Darkwoods forever?" Fang simply shook his head and patted my shoulder.

"Got some help out." Manifesto turned a quizzical eye too me but didn't say anything and simply turned away too help other guests. I didn't ask about what just happened I was just too tired. But I found Fang explaining too me that a Faolon was another sort of werewolf. I wanted too question why no one cared that he was around and how they didn't want Fang near the village, but the smell of the food in front of me made my stomach rumble again. I nibbled on the cheeses and saw that Fang was making short work of it. I grabbed what I wanted and allowed him too eat most of it.

"How can you eat so fast?" I asked he shrugged with a mouth full of bread, after swallowing; he just sipped his mead and smiled. I figured he was hungry after fighting, soon our 'house specials' came, they seemed too be a thick stew, that when I put my spoon in too it, it stood up on its own. Fang, not seeming to really notice my inquisitive expression just ate it. I followed his example; he was of course done before me. Manifesto came back and gave us the bill, it was scribbled on a small piece of paper, and I pulled out the rumpled pound notes from my pocket and placed them on the table. Fang gave me an odd look, and shoved them back at me.

"Those won't work here . . . whatever they are . . . these will though." he said, and pulled out an actual gold coin. My mouth gapped as he set it on the table, and we took our leave.

"Why won't my money work here?" I asked, as we walked away from the Slaughtered Lamb.

"Well, they use gold and silver here, not paper." he said, as he pulled out a couple more gold and silver coins from his pocket. I didn't question it, soon we went looking for a place selling tents, and then I would be on my way home.

6

Traveling in Tents

LOOKING ABOUT THE town of Sharn, I wondered too myself of the different things that might be lurking about the corners of this world. Fang didn't seem too notice much of anything as we strolled about the town, I figured it was the alcohol in him. Soon we found a little odds and ends store. Entering the tiny area we gazed about and saw a goat looking old man standing behind a counter, we inquired about a tent. After a second of thought he turned around and grabbed a little package off of the shelving. Upon paying with more of Fang's money, (I felt bad for using it) we headed out of the store and wandered away from Sharn.

"What exactly will I be doing anyway?" I asked, as we made our way too the large lush field that was soon turning different colors with the descending light, Fang shrugged a little.

"Actually, I am not too sure, I don't know magick chica . . ." – he had gone back too calling me pet names – "I think that you just have too concentrate upon the energy and simply push it through the tent. Then I think it does the rest . . . I might be wrong though." with the fading light I noticed he was blushing. Was he embarrassed about not knowing magick? I didn't even know it myself, he was an interesting fellow, and sometimes it was hard too read him. Finally we set up the tent. It took a little time, seeing as I hadn't been camping sense I was a child and Fang clearly didn't understand the instructions. He stared at the paper, looking at the pictures,

"I think that goes there?" he stammered, as I pulled the paper away from him and simply told him what too do. It went smoother after that.

36

Staring at the tiny green camping tent (not much different then the one that Juniper had brought me in) we unzipped the flap and went in. I was amazed that there were blankets upon the floor of it. Fang simply told me it was enchanted and left it at that.

"It's up too you now." he told me, I sat before him, his bulkier frame taking up most of the sitting room. Closing my eyes I concentrated upon the energy and said a little prayer too whoever might be listening for guidance. The soft golden glow pushed through my veins; I felt the magick shift as darkness surrounded the tent. The flow didn't seem as powerful or as fast as Junipers, I voiced this too Fang.

"She's over three thousand years old . . . at least, she has a leg up on us luv. We'll get there; it will just probably take longer. Like a night or so?" his voice was questioning, I had no answer for him, I lay down and stared up at the roof of the tent. My body was tired, but my mind was wide awake.

"Fang, tell me a little more . . . on what it's like too be a Werewolf?" I guess my question must have startled him for he didn't answer for a few heart beats. Lying down besides me, he put his arms under his head, and also fixed his gaze upon the ceiling.

"Its hard too explain, as I've told you, it's a power, a power you can control after a while, but when it first happens. You wake up thinking you have become possessed or something. You're afraid, wandering about for answers. I was lucky, I ran in too another werewolf shortly after becoming one. He explained so much too me . . ." he paused and sighed, his eyes flicking to me then back too their original spot. "You realize you cant return to anything that is normal, and once you first shift, on you're first full moon, it's the scariest thing that will ever happened too you. You feel this power over taking you're mind, then everything is clips and images, blood and gore. Then you wake up covered in blood, naked and alone . . ." he stopped and didn't say anymore. I let it slide for a bit, after a second he looked back at me. "Do you want too know how I became a werewolf?" he asked, his eyes serious, no playfulness was left in them. I nodded my head, my mouth was too dry too speak, I allowed him too talk.

"I was eighteen; I was in love with the most gorgeous girl I had ever met. And she loved me, a poor orphan who was raised by his brother, and she, so full of potential and life. I was going too ask her to be my wife. Cause that's what ya did back then, you got married young and had lots of kids too carry on you're trade. My brother and I owned a little Inn, so Ruby, the girl of my dreams, and I would have run it with Thomas . . ." His eyes grew sad, a faint glimmer of tears on his lids. "We went too a lake that night the moon was full and beautiful, I was going too ask her too be mine forever. But then it happened so fast. A creature so horrible came out. It killed her, it ripped her heart out of her chest and all I could do was sit there. Like a stupid blighter. Then it turned its eyes on me, it bit me, then I woke up and everything was different. I was a demon . . . I couldn't go back too Thomas . . . and Ruby was dead . . ." a single tear slid down his cheek as he turned his head away from me. I found that tears had traced lines down my face as well. I lay there, digesting the information given too me. Fang had been in love, and because of a werewolf she was dead and him cursed forever.

"Is . . . there a way too break a werewolves curse?" I asked, he turned back too me, his eyes dry now, and simply shook his head; he turned his face away again.

"I shouldn't have told you that . . . I'm sorry." he stammered as he sat up and gazed down at me. I pushed my self up in a sitting position.

"No, its good too know, you're my friend . . . and I guess I would of heard it eventually . . . I'm sorry." I whispered the apology, a smile played upon his lips.

"Don't be, I haven't told that story for a long time . . . I think about them, wondering what it would have been like too have been human . . . but then I come back here. And at least I have a friend like you now." the smile spread and soon the tears were forgotten. We continued too talk through the slow moving darkness. I discovered a lot about Fang, including that he had a doctors knowledge for the dark ages, not really something one could use now but it was neat too know. He also wanted too learn things so badly, I quickly was trying too fill him in on as much as I could about the mortal realm. Which he wanted too know how it had changed. It was hard too explain cars and other things like that to him, but he seemed too grasp most of it.

"So their like carriages?" Fang asked, propping his head up with an arm, I laughed a little, I was attempting too explain how almost everyone used cars.

"Yea I guess you can say that, but they have motors in them and they drive around just because you push little peddles." I told him, he nodded, taking it in.

"The mortal realm sounds really weird now . . . no gambling houses, no brothels, are there still pubs lining the streets?" he asked, I shook my head, making a disgruntled face he flipped over and laid on his back.

"And you live in it . . . I can't imagine. You seem so sweet and nice, but no, you're just a crazy girl . . ." he trailed off when I gave him an odd look, he smiled. "A nice girl, but crazy I bet ya. You must have boys lining up too take you out every night." he said, we had talked about modern dating, even though I wasn't an expert, I told him the date mainly consisted of dinner and a movie. Then I had to explain movies, and he found all of that very knowledgeable. A light blush crept over my face; I had actually never been on a date.

"Um . . . no . . . I don't . . . I've never had anything like that." I whispered for I knew he could hear me. Lifting his eyebrows he stared at me for a bit.

"Well their stupid aren't they. A cute thing like you and no guys wanting too whisk ya away? Their all gits." I found myself laughing at this, Fang's eyes softened and he propped himself up again and stared at me.

"I'm serious; you're a sweet girl, why haven't you been on a date? Hell even I've been on dates . . . not modern ones, but dates . ." his voice grew quite and sad, I wondered what was going on through his head, but he quickly lay back down and showed no sign of the sadness anymore.

"I just never have, I always worked or wanted too get better in school. Or was helping my Grandma . . . I never thought about it, I am after all only eighteen." when I said this, Fang looked back at me.

"I was going too marry a girl when I was eighteen." he whispered, I tried too speak but words wouldn't come too me. The idea of loosing someone that close too myself, it made my eyes tear up, Fang noticed.

"Oh don't cry luv, I didn't mean too get you upset." he trailed a finger on my cheek catching a tear. He stared long and hard at it, and put his hand down. I felt my face growing red again. I turned my body away from him, and let my thoughts wander for a second. What was it like too love someone that you would actually want too spend the rest of you're life with them. I heard Fang shifting besides me. Then I felt a strong arm wrap around me.

"Don't be angry at me." he whispered as he hugged me. My body held still, he thought I was angry at him? I pushed myself up and looked down at him, his face held concern.

"I am not mad at you; I was just thinking . . . what is it like . . . to be in love?" I asked him, after a second of thought he sat up as well, and shrugged a little.

"It's hard to describe. It's amazing, you feel whole, and like everything has a meaning and a purpose. I knew exactly what I was going too do, and how our lives would have been. But then its tragic . . . it can be taken away so fast." his voice cracked a little, as thoughts drifted through his face and eyes. I let him sit in his reveries, I wanted too know that feeling. I had at least a friend now, but I wanted a whole and meaningful life. Would I get that now that I was an Earth Guardian? Fang brought me back when he yawned and stretched.

"Well, maybe we should sleep; you never know where we might turn up in the morning. G'night chica." he said, flopping over and grabbing a blanket for himself. I wanted too laugh, but I held it back, laying down I pulled a blanket up over me. Closing my eyes I allowed all of my thoughts too slowly drift through my mind . . .

"Ruby . . ." I felt hot breath on my neck, my eyes opened, Fang was curled up beside me, an arm around my torso and his face pressed up against my neck. I tried to squirm away, but he tightened his grip on me. Sighing, I pushed my free hand against his forehead, trying to wake him. With a start he opened his eyes they glowed a fierce yellow at me, he growled, blinking slowly he stopped. His eyes faded back too green, my whole body was tense.

"Sorry . . ." he whispered as he scooted away from me. I let out a slow breath of air.

"It's alright; you were just um . . . well squishing me?" I didn't know how else too describe it, Fang let out a short laugh that almost sounded like a bark.

"That's all?" he asked, I felt my face grow red, he was so casual about things that I would of never tolerated back home.

"I've been alone for a long time luv . . ." his voice grew quite, he took in a long breath and let it out slowly. "I've always been around others, when I was little, my brother was always there. When I was part of the Daligulven's pack . . . I was always with my friends. Then I was put in the Darkwoods, I've been alone, so I am sorry. You're just the warmest thing I've been around for a while." I felt bad, his voice was so authentic, I didn't want him too get the wrong impression from being close too me though.

"I am the total opposite; I've always pretty much been alone. I had my Grandma yes, but she was old and once I turned fifteen I was allowed too live on my own. I've never had a family, so, I am sorry if I am cold too you." I said it before I even thought it, I felt my ears burn, I had never told anyone that, I had always kept too myself. Why did I find myself talking too him so easily. That question was easily answered, he had saved my life, and he had helped me so much. Tilting my head in thought, I let them drain away from me; Fang was still and silent as he stared at me.

"Let's just try and get some sleep okay?" I finally said, he agreed, we lay back down and again dreams over took me.

The Demon was before me, its face bathed in crimson . . . of blood . . . my blood, and its breath was hot on my face. Something burned within me. Then there was light, so bright it burnt through me in too my very mind. Then someone was there, someone trying to tear me away, away from everything that I barely knew. I screamed once more . . .

Someone was holding me, and shushing me.

"Keara, luv, stop it you'll hurt yourself!" Fang's voice was trembling; he was holding me like a child. I had tears upon my face; my hands were up on my chest. I had been ripping at the skin near my throat. My voice was hoarse as I let out a groan. It had felt so real.

"Are you alright? You kept screaming, I didn't know what to do?" his voice was quite, he held on too me, I noticed I was in his lap. My mind chorused with the events in my dreams, something had killed me there.

"Oh God . . . That creature . . ." I finally managed too whisper, Fang didn't ask, he allowed me too shake, as I felt the tension ease from my muscles.

"It was a dream, I was being killed, it was on me, and attacking me . . . I couldn't get away." I whispered, Fang watched me closely, his green eyes full of emotions that I couldn't understand.

"Nightmares are never fun . . . how's you're throat?" he asked, I put a hand on the bruising flesh, luckily my nails weren't long, so it didn't hurt too badly.

"I think I am okay." finally my eyes had focused all the way, and there was light coming through the slits of the tent.

"Did we stop?" I whispered Fang nodded.

"That's why I didn't want you screaming, I tried to wake you up, but you were going crazy. You almost punched me in the face when I was trying to calm ya down. Luckily you're not that strong." he smiled, I found myself smiling back, he seemed too always make everything better. Fang set me down on the blankets; I straightened up and reached for the zipper of the tent. Finally we would find out where we were, and if I was any closer on going home.

7

In the Now

THE SUN LIGHT was harsh as we stepped out, we were in another field but it was by many different houses. Spotting a young girl taking a small dog for a walk, I sprinted up too her and asked her where we were. She gave me an odd look, and stared at Fang, she couldn't have been more then twelve but she blushed, as Fang smiled at her. The dog she was leading growled loudly at him, Fang only stared at it, a low growl rumbling in his throat. Luckily the girl didn't hear it.

"You're in Newberg . . . what did you do just pop out of the Earth." she asked, her American accent very thick, Fang started too speak but I stopped him.

"Um no . . . we're just a bit lost that's all. Where's the nearest bank?" I asked, again Fang stared at me, not understanding, I hadn't explained banks too him yet.

After describing a route too the closest bank, we headed off Fang finally asked where we were going.

"I have no American dollars. I only have Pound notes, so I need too get us some money if we are going too be able too figure anything out." I pointed out too him, he shrugged, and stretched his arms up. Making our way through a neighborhood of homes, we finally found a main street; the cars zoomed by us, making Fang almost jump out of his skin.

"You didn't say they would be this loud." he said, glaring at the noisy metal beasts that zipped by us. I shook my head and continued too walk. Upon reaching the bank, I discovered the date was only about a week after I had left England with Juniper. Standing in line, I quickly remembered my account information, I figured I could get more money wired too us, we finally made our way too the front desk. The tired looking women had me fill out various forms, as I explained that we had just gotten off a plane too visit a sick relative so we needed money. She didn't seem too even listen too the story that I had just pulled out of my brain. She handed me about four hundred dollars worth of small bills (living alone I had a lot saved up for a rainy day), I handed Fang about fifty dollars. He blinked at it and put it in his pocket of rather dirty looking pants. I stared down at our clothing; they were grubby and had dark stains of Fang's blood on it. After leaving the bank, I walked along the main strip of the tiny town of Newberg. A car pulled up too us, a young man was in it, he must have been in his college years.

"Need a lift?" he asked, apparently we looked as though we needed it, I thanked him and asked him how close a clothing store was. He said about two miles. Not feeling up too walking that far with the cars following us, we hopped in with the mysterious youth. Fang just simply glared at the fellow.

"What's wrong?" I asked him as we were securely in the back seat of the man's sedan.

"He's a vampire." he whispered, my jaw dropped at him, then I turned too the man, he looked back and nodded.

"You're friend is right. But don't get the wrong impression, I am trying to help. You looked lost, and I could tell by you're aura's on what you both are." he said, as he flipped off the music that had been playing. I nodded and felt stupid for not even noticing it. The word aura rang through my mind; I had heard it before from venders in London. They would say it was the light and energy that was radiated from people. I guess they were right, sense I got my new sight I could see this light on everyone I met.

"How could you tell?" I asked Fang, he smiled a little and turned too me.

"Well he had a very slow heart rate, and he smells like rank dirt." he said, loud enough for the vampire too hear, the man looked back and just smiled.

"Werewolves are very racist people aren't they? By the way, the name is Arez" he said a smirk lining his face, upon further examination he did have paler skin, and his eyes were jet black, and a hint of sharp teeth showed when he smiled. I introduced Fang and myself.

"I thought Vampires couldn't go in the sunlight?" I asked, Arez laughed.

"We can, we just can't stay out too long it makes us weak. But I was just out on a cruise when I noticed ya. Oh here we are." he said, pulling up too a large retail store, by the name of Fred Meyers. We exited, I thanked Arez, and he said not too mention it, and then sped away.

"You are an odd Earth Guardian, first you make friends with an Aukoc, and then you take rides from Vampires. Whatever will they think of you?" Fang mocked, I jabbed him a bit in the stomach, and started too walk towards the large store. Fang's body movement became tense as we weaved our way through the crowds in the store.

"What's come over you?" I asked him finally, when he kept jumping as people passed him. Speaking low, he finally whispered too me.

"I haven't been this close too so many people for three hundred years . . . its so weird . . . they all smell so different, its hard too breath." his voice was hoarse as he said it, I didn't ask him too explain anymore. We finally made it too the back and found the men's clothing.

"I have no idea what size you are . . . so I guess we'll just figure it out by trial and error." I said, I went through clothes for Fang, who tried too help but also didn't know his size and kept holding up rather strangely patterned pants, I found him clothes that I hoped would fit him. Pushing him in too the dressing rooms, I told him too wait a little bit then try on the clothes. I went off and found a pair of dark jeans, and a red shirt that looked like they would fit and went back too the dressing rooms. Where Fang was standing wearing his new clothes. The pants fit him well, and the shirt he liked because it was tight, I didn't say anything. The modern pants were a dark brown color, and the shirt was a lighter blue with a dark blue stripe on the chest. I told him too go back in and change, and I found my own dressing room. And put on the new clothes, they fit well enough. I heard Fang's voice.

"This place is weird, There's a sign in here that has pictures of funny shorts on It." he shouted, I called back too him.

"That's a chart of men's underwear styles I guess." I said calmly, I couldn't believe I was having this conversation, and then I heard something that almost made me fall over laughing with embarrassment.

"What's underwear?" he asked, I coughed, and left the dressing room, making him stay there, finding a pair of boxers I threw them over the stall wall.

"Wear those under you're pants. Please." I put in, luckily no one really seemed too notice our odd conversation; finally he came out, holding his new clothing. Finding a check out line, I bought the clothes and I went in too the bathroom too change, Fang tried too follow.

"No go in there." I said pointing too the men's bathroom, he didn't ask why, he just obeyed. I felt bad for him, he didn't understand so much. He must be very confused. Changing I felt better and cleaner, I exited, Fang was standing outside waiting for me, we then dumped our old blood stained tattered clothes in the trash and headed out in too the world again. After wandering about a bit, we finally made our way in the general area of where we had left the tent. Fang's head perked up.

"Music?" he said, I couldn't hear anything, and then he started walking in a random direction.

After a few more blocks I started too hear the music as well, it was loud and happy.

"Their must be a carnival going on." I told him, tilting his head he continued too walk towards the sounds. Upon entering a very large field by a small school, we noticed the large carnival, there were about six rides, and various venders and games placed about. Fang's eyes got very large as he watched a small roller coaster, and a larger thing called the yo-yo, which was a large contraption where you sat in swings and got spun around.

"Can we?" he asked, his excitement bubbling forward, I nodded and we found a ticket vender, after getting the tickets, Fang started too pull me towards all of the different rides. He wanted too go on one called the zipper, it was large and you were placed in a cage and got spun upside down. I went on it with him, after feeling sick too my stomach, we stumbled out, Fang was teetering from side too side.

"That was fun!" he said, and ran towards another ride, trying to keep up with him, the crowd closed around me, I couldn't see him.

"Fang?" I called, he didn't answer. After another second of looking, I felt a hand grip my arm, I whipped around and stared in too ice blue eyes. Juniper's loud voice whispered too me.

"Why hello there. Come and sit with Me." she said, and pulled me over too a bench, plopping down, I did the same, staring at her blankly I watched as she nibbled on a corndog that she was carrying.

"Such strange food, well . . . you found a carnival, how sweet . . . showing the Aucok a nice time before I kill him?" Cold fear gripped my stomach.

"You Can't . . ." I managed too stammer out, Juniper's eyes narrowed at me as she threw the corndog away.

"Oh I can . . . and I will, he's a killer, and he's done horrible things . . . and needs too be punished." her anger flared around me, I could feel it emanating from her like a wave of heat.

"Please don't, he's not bad . . . I swear, I'll watch over him, he will be my responsibility." Her glare got worse, I wanted to shrink away, but the bench was too small.

"Damn you . . . fine . . . I can't go against that, hell I set up that rule . . . if you want too baby sit him go ahead. But if he kills ONE innocent soul, I will make sure you are punished as well . . . besides that, I am impressed you got out alive. Here are your instructions, until later girly . . ." she vanished right there, I sat staring at the rolled up parchment on the seat next too me that had appeared after she left. After a second I heard Fang's voice by me.

"Where have you been? What's wrong?" he asked, when I turned too him, he looked at the parchment that was by me, walking over he picked it up and handed it too me. My hands were shaking, as I opened it, he sat down besides me. I read it, letting the words sink in too my mind

Dear Keara:

Sense you have gotten out of the Darkwoods, a tutor will be appointed to you. After returning too England, he will meet you in you're flat. After that you will be allowed too participate as an Earth Guardian, on the council. Upon that time you will be given different tasks for you're continent. Enjoy you're time.

Enclosed is one plane ticket too England, use it well.

– Earth Guardian Council . . .

Gulping in the fresh air around me, the noises of the Carnival faded around me, only Fang's presence and the parchment in my hands meant anything too me.

"You have too go back . . ." he whispered, there was a sadness in his voice.

"What do you mean 'me', you're coming too aren't you?" I asked him, my voice was small and shaky, and I couldn't imagine going back without him. He shook his head, a glimmer of something was passing through his eyes I bit my lip, trying to suppress the feelings of being lost.

"Why?" I whispered, he put an arm around me, I didn't fight it.

"I can't go back, I grew up there, I hunted and killed there . . . I can't now . . . give me time and I might be able too. But not now, I like it here, its nice. I think I could live here for a little bit. But you have too go back." he said, his voice was monotone as he spoke, I looked at him, that cold fear crept in too me again.

"I can't just leave you here, you don't know how too read, you don't know this world." I told him, he simply nodded his head.

"No but I'll have you're help. You told me a lot . . . I think I can manage it a bit without you. I survived in the Darkwoods for three hundred years, I could wait a bit longer too go back too England."

We left the carnival; the fun of the day was slipping away. We walked back towards the retail store, for there was a motel up there. We found the place and I got us a room for the night. Upon entering it, I sat down on one of the queen sized beds, Fang sat on the other we didn't speak I just kept staring at the ticket in my hands. I could go back, I would be trained as an Earth Guardian, and maybe I would even write this whole crazy story down or something like it, and get it published. Fang finally spoke first.

"At least you'll get trained in you're magick, I couldn't help ya with that." he said. I nodded, and bit my lips again.

"I think I am going too shower." I whispered, as I went in too the bathroom and started the hot shower. I sat under the blazing water, and allowed it too take the dirt from my body. I felt tears trickle down my face. Why was I crying? I was going

JOURNEY THROUGH THE DARK WOODS | 47

home . . . but what about Fang . . . ? My tears went away, as I got out of the shower and dried, I heard a knock on the door.

"Um . . . you okay?" Fang's voice asked, I told him yes, and quickly got back in too some clothes, I pulled my hair up in too a towel.

"You can come in." I told him, the door opened, Fang stood there, staring at me, I smiled at him, and a small smile crept up on his face.

"Have enough time too think and all that?" he asked, I nodded and went about exiting the bathroom.

"One sec . . . can you show me how too use this thing." he asked pointing at the shower; I showed him the handles and how too get it warm and told him too dry off with the towels. I felt him alone and sat on the bed again, staring at a spot on the wall.

I had too go back too England, this tutor could teach me all of my magick, but then there was Fang. He didn't have money; he didn't have a job, what would he do? I mulled over more thoughts. I could write again and get something published, and maybe get my life back on track. The bathroom door opened and Fang came out, his hair still a bit wet and plastered too his head instead of looking shaggy like normal, his ears poked through, I made a mental note that they were pointed. Maybe it was another werewolf thing, I decided not too ask.

"That thing is nice. When I was little no one got that clean, nice feeling that is." he said, sitting down on the bed besides me, he looked as content as a cat with cream. Smiling at his comment, I agreed with him, I didn't want too think of a time when one couldn't take a hot shower. I looked at the phone on the bed stand and picked it up. Fang watched me as I hit the zero button.

"Room service." a none descript male voice echoed.

"Ello, this is room 120, and I would like some dinner."

"Okay ma'am what would you like?"

"Um . . . soup and salad, I don't care on kinds really, and a roast beef sandwich with all of the fixings." there was a pause and the voice said it would be up in half an hour. Fang's eyes were wide.

"How did you do that?" he asked, I explained about phones, and after a bit our food arrived, Fang finished off his before I even got too my salad.

After a good meal, we finally told ourselves it was time for sleep, I crawled in too one of the queen size beds. Fang sat down on the one across from me.

"Um . . . Fang . . . in the morning, do you want me too help you figure out where and how you will live here?" I asked him, he nodded, and flopped down and crawled under the blankets.

"These are soft." he whispered, I laughed a little, and dreams took me over and no nightmares threatened my mind.

8

Finding Herself

UPON AWAKING THE next morning, it turned out too be a slightly over cast and a saddening day. I knew by the end of it all I would have to leave this nice little town. And Fang. I shook the thoughts from my head; as we headed back off to the bank too exchange the gold and silver that Fang had brought with him in too American money. Luckily they did have a money changer for this sort of thing and stared in awe at the purity of the metals. We finally left with a large amount of money in Fang's pockets.

After looking through various apartments all walking distance from restaurants and stores, we gave up for a bit and found a place to eat. It was a nice Chinese Restaurant called Lucky Fortune, Fang was delighted too try new things.

"How will you get back too England? Magick?" Fang asked over his spicy soup, which made his cheeks red. Putting down an egg roll I had been nibbling on I attempted too explain planes too him.

"So big flying things of metal . . . interesting, how will you get too an air pot?" he questioned, I corrected him and told him I would hop a bus most likely, he nodded, and we continued too eat our meal. Leaving the restaurant, I found a small bus stop by a store, and started too read the times of departure.

"This should take me too the Airport . . . good thing I got out money." I whispered, seeing that a bus was coming in about a half an hour. Fang nodded solemnly, sitting down on the bench we discussed over and over again what he would do when he got an apartment.

"I think I got it, make sure I make up a story about how I am hitch hiking and don't have an ID . . . and tell them I'll pay 'em in cash . . . sounds easy enough. And for money I'll figure out something." he said trying too reassure me, a coldness was still gnawing at my gut.

"That sounds about right, and I showed you how too use the pay phones, just use them too call me." I handed him a piece of paper with my telephone number on it with the extensions too Europe.

"It should work out fine luv I'll call you tomorrow when I know you'll be home. And hopefully by then I will have a place. And if not I can always sleep in the woods or something. I am really used too that." he told me, smiling, giving him a weak smile we waited in silence for a bit longer. Then the bus lumbered up, and opened its door too me. As I got up, Fang reached for me, and caught me in a large hug.

"Don't be worried. I'll be fine, keep an eye out." he whispered, as I felt tears slide down my face, trying too make this as easy as possible, I hopped on too the bus and sat down. I stared at the window, Fang watched me leave, and at first I thought I saw tears in his eyes as well.

The plane ride had been hard, I was tempted too just run back too him, and stay in America. But I knew I had to face my training. Upon returning home, I found another mysterious note, saying how my trainer would be over by the end of the week. Chewing on my lip I reached for the phone and dialed my grandmother's number. Her gravely voice came over the receiver

"'Ello?" she asked, a cough followed. Clearing my throat I responded.

"Grandmother . . . it's me Keara." I said formally, she chuckled.

"Oh dear, I thought you had dropped off the face of the planet."

"You wont believe how close you are on that one Gran . . . can I come over tonight?"

She agreed and had to hang up because of a coughing fit. I tried to keep my mind occupied with other things until that evening came. After a boring wait I went over too the nursing home she was staying at.

The nursing home smelled of flowers and disinfectant, heading up too her room, I knocked lightly on the door, I heard her beckon me in.

"So nice too see you dearie, how are things?" she asked, her face was wrinkled and her bright brown eyes shown through too me, her hair was silvered and fell down on her shoulders. She lay in a bed with a chair near it. Sitting upon the chair, I put my hands in my lap and looked down.

"Gran . . . I need too ask you some questions." I told her. Grandma looked away, and stared out the window that over looked a garden.

"Juniper took you didn't she?" her voice was quiet, I couldn't help it I jumped up, and stared at her in disbelief so many questions ran through my mind.

"Please sit down luv, I have a long story too tell you." I sat down and watched her, wanting her too explain more.

"It happened not too long ago, about eighty years ago. I was once an Earth Guardian, I had passed through the Darkwoods just as you have just done. I was even helped by a nice werewolf chap." – A blush crept over my cheeks, but she didn't seem too notice and continued – "After being trained, and about eighteen years ago, I was up in Scotland, when a vampire group attacked a families home. I went and stopped them, but I was almost too late. The parents had been killed, slaughtered like animals. But then there was a small baby, she was so innocent, just a couple of weeks old. She was almost dead as well; I could feel her soul slipping away." Pausing she sniffed lightly and suppressed a cough. "And in that moment I realized what I had to do. I gave her half my soul, she lived, but I started too age. I caught up with my actual age, and that's why I am old now. Giving that child half my soul, which I found out, also had most of my magick in it, made me not be immortal anymore. So I raised that child . . . you see, that's why you have no parents, they were killed by Vampires so long ago." her voice grew still as she coughed in too a tissue. I stared at her, my mind racing. I would have died if this woman hadn't saved me. She wasn't really my grandma? But she had raised me that had too count for something. I looked away, tears welling up in my eyes.

"I had nightmares there . . . in the Darkwoods, are they because of my past?" I asked my voice shaking and my eyes still wet. Setting her hands in her lap she tried too smile at me, but it faltered.

"Maybe, I am not even sure on how I saved you . . . those nightmares could be from memories I passed too you with my soul . . ." the coughing started up again, she brought the tissue up too her mouth, but I could see the trace of blood on her lips. My throat and chest knotted with tension.

"I am going too die Keara . . . most likely tonight. All I can say to you is trust you're teacher, and follow you're heart." more tears sprang from my eyes as I looked at the women who had sacrificed so much so that I could live.

"But why me?" I asked, she smiled, a glimmer of tears on her old eyes.

"I knew you would do great things . . . and you will. Go home Keara. Go and be happy, learn well and live well." I said my final farewells to my grandma, when I got home; I heard the phone ring and picked it up. It was a woman from the nursing home; Ehlorra had passed away about half an hour after I left. I sank down and cried, I cried for the women who had saved me and raised me. The one who had given me this life.

After another hour or so, another call came through my phone; there were still tears in my eyes. I picked up the phone.

"Hey, I got this thing too work, how was you're flight?" it was Fang's beaming voice; I felt more tears slide down my face.

"It was good . . ." I said in a hoarse choking voice. I found myself telling him that my Grandma had passed, but I didn't tell me what she had told me. I didn't feel it mattered. She was my Grandma in all respects, almost a mother. And she had allowed me too live.

"I am so sorry luv, I wish I was there . . ." he whispered, I knew he was sad for me, but I didn't want him too be sad. I started too change the topic, and found out that he had found an apartment where he could stay. He was happy about this and figured he could do odd chores for people too get money, I liked the idea.

After more then an hour of talking, we soon said our good byes. I sat down on the edge of my love seat, and stared off in too the growing darkness. My life was about to get more interesting, I just knew it.

9

The End of Thoughts

"YOU'RE NOT CONCENTRA-TING." a harsh voice said behind me, I was sitting cross legged in the middle of my living room.

"I am trying too Master Raven . . . I really am." I said, my new teacher, was a middle aged man, who had the strong feel of power about him. He had dark brown hair that hung down too his shoulders. And vivid deep blue eyes, he walked around too look at me.

"You are thinking of other things. If you don't perform this spell correctly it take most of you're energy and most likely kill you." he warned me, I knew he was just being dramatic but I still tried harder, I felt the energy pulse around me, as I pulled through it with my own power.

"Answer my heed! Follow my prayers . . . bring forth you're light!" I screamed, as a bright form grew before me, it twinkled and died out. I slumped back, all of my own energy drained out of me.

"Good, you did well bringing the Light elemental, tomorrow we will practice on keeping one here for more then a second. But you are doing well." he said, sitting down in front of me, he handed me a glass of water. I drank deeply and set it down in front of me.

"Thank you . . . I am sorry my mind was wandering." I whispered, I reached behind my back and grabbed an apple from a tray and bit in too it. With using magick I had to eat at random times too keep up my bodies energies.

52

"It's alright child, you did well. And I know you were thinking of the Aukoc." Raven's eyes were bright with an unknown knowledge, I almost chocked on the apple.

"How did you . . . ?" I asked he put his hand up, silencing me.

"I read you're file, yes you have a file child. Everyone whom works with the council does. And I heard about the Aukoc Silver Fang whom helped you out of the Darkwoods . . . he means a lot too you doesn't he?" he asked, a blush crept over my face, I had only known Master Raven for about half a month now. And after this month I would be on my own for learning magicks.

"I suppose he does . . . he is one of my only friends." I whispered he nodded.

"All I can tell you is do what is best, follow you're feelings child, you cant go wrong with it." he told me, a hidden sadness showed in his eyes, tilting my head, I asked about the emotions being conveyed.

"Did you ever have a friend who the council didn't like?" I asked I knew that Juniper hated Fang with a passion. But I always wondered why the council had to hate him as well.

"Yes I did . . . I loved a vampire once. She was a good woman, and didn't prey upon humans. But the council wouldn't listen to Me." he said his eyes lost in memories.

"What happened to her?" I asked quietly bringing him back to the present.

"The Council killed her, that was nearly twenty years ago, and I continued too train the young Earth Guardians. I am under their service until they don't need me. I have no choice in it." he stood up, and showed me a rare smile. "Practice you're magick, I will be back tomorrow. You better meditate tonight. And remember, follow you're heart and feelings." he said as he disappeared.

My training followed like that, once a day Master Raven would arrive in my home for five hours of magick work. He gave me many books; I had to buy another book shelf because of it. But even with all of the magick I was learning, my mind would always return too Fang. He had settled in too his apartment, and was having fun doing chores for strangers for money. He would call me about once a day on the pay phones. I wanted too visit him soon, but my publisher finally had called me and wanted a story from me. So with my training and my writing I was quite busy and would be so for a couple of months.

I would assure Fang that soon I would fly out there and see him. Or if my magick was good enough by then I would teleport myself there. That would be cheaper, I had thought too myself as I had a simple breakfast and waited for Master Raven too arrive. He seemed too like too stop by in the mornings. I was happy with my life, I had a great friend, and I was doing something with my existence. And soon I would be going too the council like a real Earth Guardian, once Raven was done training me that is. I smiled as the sun light filled my flat. Everything was getting better for me.

PART 2

PREFACE

*WOULD I TAKE it all back, if I could?
I don't think I would. Just the very
thought of not knowing her face, her beauty, her scent . . . Lavender and basil, like a fresh
garden in a sacred place, where only the purest of souls can rest . . .*

*And where demons like myself should never interrupt, else the very Lord of this world
would smite my body and curse my soul . . .*

1

Fang

YAWNING AT THE dimly lit room, I shuddered in the cold air, getting up I flipped the lights on. The small room had barely anything in it, a small bed, a dresser, and a tiny writing desk, that I never used. Shuffling out of the bedroom, my feet hit the cold wood flooring, grimacing, I made my way to the kitchen, only to reveal that most of the food was gone. Grumbling about getting around to buying groceries, I made my way to the living room, and flopped down on the lumpy bedraggled sofa. Flicking through the channels of a small television set, my mind wandered amongst the going-ons of the world. Nothing took my interest, finally, unsatisfied with the television, my feet took me too the bathroom. Warming the shower up, I quickly took off the little clothing I was wearing and amerced myself in the hot water that feel from the nozzle. The knowledge of hygiene was amazing in this day of age, soaps that were just for your hair, or for your face, even some just for your body were available too everyone. I had only been out of the Darkwoods for seven months but already the thought of not showering at least every two days made my nose wrinkle.

Exiting from the shower squeaky clean, I toweled off, pulling it around my waist, I extracted a comb from the sinks counter, then examined myself in the mirror. Straggly unruly dirty blonde hair that never tolerated a comb until coming too this world tugged and pulled at my scalp as I managed to comb through it. Pale emerald eyes watched skillfully as I put the instrument down, a thick garish scar covered my left eyebrow to my eye. I wasn't very ordinary looking, most thought me quite handsome, with high cheek bones and a roman nose that set my face off quite nicely. My skin had a natural tan sheen about it but the only things marring it were random scars covering my back and some on my chest and arms. I didn't appear to look eighteen anymore, I had aged, in some form or fashion, and looked well over twenty five. I had once been told that depending on your tribe, you aged according to a set limit, for example every two hundred years, one year would show on your face. I myself had no idea what aging I had, but I definitely wasn't eighteen anymore. This helped, for in this world, you had to be over twenty-one to do anything. Stretching to my full height, which was about six foot, I made my way back to my bedroom to put on clean clothes.

A black t-shirt, a rough pair of Levis, and some sneakers later, I emerged from my apartment refreshed and curious. I was learning everything at once. This new world held challenges, like cars, you can't chase them and they can hurt you, was one such challenge. Walking down stairs (my apartment was on the top floor of only two stories), to the street level of the small apartment complex that only held about twenty apartments. Which all faced a large parking lot and on the far side was a large wooded area that joggers used. I waved to my elderly landlady whom couldn't even see two feet in front of her. I hadn't even seen people over sixty until getting out of the Darkwoods, it was weird too see what old age could do too people. Walking along the sidewalk, I noticed no one was really out at this early morning; it was a weekday so most people went to work. I worked whenever people wanted me too. It was sort of nice. Passing by the local elementary school, which was just off of ninth street and fairly close too my apartment. I watched as a crusty old janitor scuffled about the play yard. School was another big thing around here, everyone had an education . . . or at least they wanted you too. I hadn't even learned too read this new English language, until I got out of the Darkwoods. It was taking time but I was coming along. Even though in my day and age, when I was a young soul, I had what my time had called an education in herbal remedies. I had a doctor's knowledge for the dark ages. But not for the 21th Century. Sighing at the thought of not having an education, another thing that Keara had, it made me wonder how she even looked at me. I was a demon from another time period that happened upon her in the Darkwoods, and she was a smart, young beautiful Earth Guardian.

"Oh how can this work?" I whispered too myself, my English accent still thick on my lips.

Casually walking to my destination, a little pay phone that was on the outskirts of a large university, I knew that the only other payphone was downtown, and didn't feel up too that walk this morning. Pulling out the coins for the device, I pushed it through the slot and punched in the numbers which I had memorized by heart.

One ring, two rings, Click.

JOURNEY THROUGH THE DARK WOODS

"Ello?" a timid English accent came over the speaker, I took a breath.

"Ello, Chica" I bellowed, just as a stuffy suit walked by my path, giving me an odd measured look.

Keara laughed. "How I've not missed that name, how are you Fang?" Telling her the boring details of my life only took a couple of minutes.

"So how is life there?"

"Well, it's fairly good right now, I am attempting to get my story published, and it should only take one more week. Then I'll get my answer from the publishers. Then I'll be heading out to your end of the world. I wish I could call you, you really do need to get a phone Fang this is so hard sometimes."

Her voice echoed in my head, as I smiled, it was hard, but I couldn't afford to get a phone, I never would tell her though. She would get in a huff and explain how she would send me money. Even though she could barely pay her own rent on what little money she got as a writer.

"Its ok pet, we can handle it, and I'll call you everyday, you know unless Juniper catches up with me and skins me alive." a small gasp came over the receiver.

"Don't joke about that Fang! It's not funny most of the time. I hate being away, but once I legitimize this deal, I can head out there and we can see where you want too live."

My heart felt like it was going to burst. The thought of seeing her, smelling her, maybe even holding her hand, being with her again, made me light headed.

"Mmm, that would be good, well girl, I have to get to my 'clients' house. So how about I call you tomorrow and we'll talk longer."

Sighing, she agreed, we said our good byes and hung up. Continuing my walk, my head whirled, a week! In a week I would know if she was coming out here finally, I had missed her so badly.

"And you won't be an idiot!" I whispered harshly too myself. I would do the right thing; I would ask her a question I had never asked anyone. I would ask her too be mine!

After working in an elderly ladies garden for the rest of the morning, I left her dainty abode in the peeking afternoon heat. Summer had come out to bite every creature in the tiny town of Newberg hard on the ass. In the baking heat I lumbered along to my tiny apartment, at least it would be cool, a slight wind washed over my sweating brow, when a scent happened across me as well. Pausing, I sniffed again. Familiar in so many ways, my brain couldn't dredge up the image that went along with this sharp musky scent. Definitely male and a werewolf. From a scent you can't get tribe or much of anything, unless you knew it very well. A low growl rose up from my throat; a passing human stared at me while his pace quickened him away. Shaking my head, I took a longer way home, but the scent followed, it tingled past me at every turn I took. My head was washed in it, finally getting to my apartment, I climbed the stairs three at a time and quickly got in too my claustrophobic space.

The scent hadn't followed me here, sighing; I sat down on the couch. Luckily the old lady whom I worked for had provided me with lunch and about a hundred dollars for my efforts. A knock came too my door, figuring it was the land lady or a curious neighbor; I swaggered over to the white door. Opening it with a small flourish my mind rattled as the scent washed over me and the person attached to the smell stood in front of me. A little shorter then me, his black hair was pulled back in a tight pony tail that fell past his shoulders, his face was angular, but not harsh, it was sturdy enough to hold all of the years that grew around his eyes. Which were the color of pale amber, an almost golden look. He smiled, I felt my jaw drop.

"Hello, Cody, it's been a long time, hasn't it?" his voice was silken with a faint accent around it, that told that when he was human he had grown up in what is now Wales. My eyes narrowed.

"What do you want Black Mist?"

2

Mist over Their Eyes

STARING IN TOO the eyes of someone whom I hadn't seen for at least four hundred years made me cringe. His golden eyes stared deeply at me.

"You really haven't changed, have you?" Black Mist whispered he still stood within the threshold of my door.

"Well, you might as well come in." Stepping aside, he entered in too the main part of the living room.

"It's small, but not as tiny as the places we used to live, eh Cody?" He always did that, a very annoying habit he had picked up from a mutual friend, he always used my human name. Taking a seat on the rumpled couch, he looked about himself.

"I didn't come here for pleasantries, there is something going on in the world, and I need your help to stop it . . . Its Kofra." That name sent shivers down my spin. She was cruel, insane and beautiful, a very deadly combination. She was the leader of a large pack of Daligulven, they were a beastly tribe of werewolves, believing that humans should be servants or killed.

"What about her? I haven't seen her sense I left the pack, and I haven't seen much of you either." I stated, blinking slowly he bowed his head.

"I'm sorry about that, I wanted too see you. But it was too risky, I was still part of that pack, I was a true member. Tara got too see you, but I could never follow her to the Darkwoods." Tara, a name that brought a sense of joy too my heart, she had been my proverbial sister, like me she was not part of the true pack, she was a Kahn, a Were tiger, with a keen know-how of magicks.

63

"Why isn't Tara here? She would have made this easier." I growled at him, her bubbling personality and how she made light of everything, would have made this simpler she would have had us laughing by now.

Black Mist shook his head, "I haven't seen her for a month she has been watching the main pack area in England."

It was at least good too hear that he was still with her in all respects, they were married, yes I know, a werewolf and a were tiger, it was an odd combination . . . but they were in love and bonded together by their souls.

"So, Kofra? What is she up too? I take it that's what you came here too tell me about. Some great plot of hers?" I mocked him, I had once looked up too him, but after he had me leave the pack, I had never quite forgiven him.

"Yes it is about her, she is making trouble, after Talon was killed, she made a plan, its something to do about the humans, and probably trying too kill them." my mind reared, Talon had been Kofra's life mate, and the other alpha of the pack . . . I had killed him. It was in the Darkwoods, when I was leading Keara out, he found me, and challenged me. Of course I fought and that's how Keara found out I was a werewolf . . . yet she never ran from me. Sighing, I let his words sink in too me. Kofra, making some master plan of vengeance, that's all I needed.

"Do you think I care? Why would I? She hated me, her plan will probably fail and she'll probably go back in too hiding for a bit. It's the same old story!" I growled, Black Mist watched me closely, no anger, no rage showed upon his cool features.

"It's not like that this time Cody, she has something guarding the pack lands that humans cant see. Red Dragons."

My breath caught in my throat, a burning image of a large beast with fiery scales and jaws that could crush a wolf's skull in less then a second. The look on my face must have been enough, Black Mist nodded.

"It's true Cody . . . she has two of them guarding the grounds. You know what happens to us when fighting one of those?" I shivered, Black Mist's voice was too calm for this sort of news, maybe things were as bad as they sounded he is the sort of person who only seeks help when things get bad.

"Well, what I've heard, mainly from Tara, is their bite is magical, and we can't heal that. Wait . . . you said Tara was around the main pack grounds! Does she know of the dragons!" my mouth became dry, if anything happened to her, my beast rose beneath my skin, sending a wave of lightening through my tendons.

"Cody, settle down! You know I could kill you if it came too that, and Tara is fine, she is smart and knows magick better then any of us." his voice again was too calm, the beast subdued, my eyes flashed a wolf's glare once more at him.

"She better be, so . . . why come too me with all of this, thinking of making a three person operation to take out Kofra?" My sarcasm dripped through my words. Again he just smiled very calmly and sat up a little straighter.

"No, I was thinking a four person operation . . . we need an Earth Guardians help on this" Ice dripped down my spine, Keara, how did he know!

JOURNEY THROUGH THE DARK WOODS

"You want me too drag Keara to a hostile place so that we can kill Kofra, and take out two dragons? No, I could never do that." I whispered the last part, Black Mist sighed. He stood up, and put his hand on my shoulder, an old gesture that I hadn't seen or felt for a long time.

"I need to go. But listen, think on it. She could help us, shear strength won't be enough, and you know only an Earth Guardians magick can defeat her. I'll be in touch." with that he was gone; I hated him for that he used to do it when we were young. I couldn't perform magick of any type; I was what they called a null for magick. Hack and slash was my ability.

"Keara . . ." I whispered in too the dark. I went back to my room, sitting down I stared in too the darkness.

Kofra, trying to finally do what every Daligulven wanted to do, destroy or enslave humans, what a happy time for me. I didn't mind humans, hell, technically Keara was human and I had been one once long ago. My life was finally getting straightened out again, I was in love, or at least I thought I was, and I was going too see the girl of my dreams very soon . . . and then Black Mist comes along. My world was tilting again, turning in too a battle, and I would have to drag Keara in too it. I would talk to her tomorrow, I had a client in the later morning, but I was an early riser, and my neighbor had free long distance minutes and a mobile phone. She said she would let me borrow it if I ever needed it, tomorrow I would need it. But what of Tara, the idea of her alone in that Daligulven infested place and dragons . . . red dragons at that, they tended to be meaner. It was hard to get dragons over too this part of the dimension. To actually transport two live red dragons to this realm certainly ordered a sentence from Juniper. But instead, it was up too Keara and me.

3

Sorting out Thoughts

RESTING MY HEAD against the still empty refrigerator, my mind chorused with the knowledge given too me. Sleep had not come easily that night, only nightmares of Black Mist from a different time, telling me I had gone too far, that the blood of an entire village was on my hands and that I would have too leave the pack. And of Kofra covered in blood laughing as she held up the body of the only girl who saw me as a person.

"It won't happen." I kept whispering too myself. With Black Mist's visit I still didn't do my grocery shopping, and it was too early in the morning to do it now. Four am, the microwave's numbers glared at me from across the kitchen. Stalking too my bedroom, I fetched some clothing that had not yet been worn and set out too find some sort of store that was open at God awful hours.

No sun shown through the morning fog that plastered themselves to the world. My weary eyes searched for any breaking of the relentless clouds that hung around me. There in the distance a thin line of pink shown over at the horizon.

"At least there'll be sun." my breath came out in a thin mist from the cold morning air, which was not touched with heat yet. Walking along the familiar side walk I happened upon a small convenient store that was alive twenty four seven. Entering the dismal place, I purchased a large pack of donuts and a Gatorade from a very tired looking Asian man. It was hard too tell where people came from, not being in the 'modern' world for over three hundred years could do that too you. Walking back to the apartment, with my breakfast slowly being eaten, the donuts churned in my stomach and the Gatorade's coolness couldn't quite quench the dryness in my throat. Dumping the food in a trash bin along the sidewalk, very rarely did a werewolf refuse a meal, I stared in too the trees marking a small wooded area used for trail walking, it also lead to my apartment. Letting my feet take me along the earthen trails my nostrils inhaled all of the morning's beauty. Small flowers lined the paths, bright blue and white, shown in the now rising sun's light. Sighing heavily, I saw no soul along the trail, no runners this early, or during the weekday's relentless drivel. Humans worked constantly, seeing all of the shops and the businesses that had erupted in this world, it felt like it had become smaller instead of bigger. Money also seemed to control the state of things. As I pondered these things something tugged on the back of my mind, like a small slap from something familiar. My head snapped up, looking around the path, I allowed my eyes to shift in to the knowing beasts, and surveyed the area. Nothing was out of the ordinary, but why did it feel like someone was watching me? Inhaling deeply no scents trailed along the air that brushed by me, except for the foliage and small animals of the woods. Shaking my head, I forced myself to relax and continue to follow the light trail before me. After another couple of minutes the same feeling crept over me.

"Who's there?" I growled low in my chest, even though my scenes weren't lying to me, I knew someone was out there.

"Hmm, still asking questions?" a light voice answered me, my mind screamed to run, to get out of this place . . . but something inside of me recognized the voice, and told me too stay.

"Who . . . Who are you?" the voice that escaped my lips was shaky.

"Can't tell, do what's right, save them." the voice whispered along my ears, as though the person was standing there, I twirled around too see if the culprit was behind me, but again no one was there. I tried to ask the voice questions, but it had vanished, my mind swirled with curiosity. To go along the wooded path some more? Or too head back to the apartments and call Keara? The latter won that one. Turning on my heels, I headed out of the mysterious place, anger bubbling under my skin, why did nothing make sense anymore!

Back at the apartment no other voices followed me and the feeling never came back. Heading up to my neighbors apartment, I tapped lightly on her door. She was generally an early riser, like me. I had met her when I moved in, she seemed nice, and she looked the age I looked. But she was purely human. We had had conversations before and even shared coffee with each other, a most vile drink that I think I will never have again. When I had told her of Keara she told me I could use her mobile phone anytime too call her with. She was a generous person.

"Coming!" her light voice shouted from the confines of her home. The door opened, and she stood in front of me, she was perfectly average, short with a plumper frame and long black hair that was pilled in a loose bun on top of her head. Her glasses were low on her nose as though she had been reading.

"Oh hello Cody, I was just reading the Newspaper, fancy you stopped by, what's the occasion?" Her American accent had a light drawl in it, and she had found the idea that I had an English accent very intriguing.

"Hi Becka, its nothing much, I was just wondering if I could use that phone of yours. I sort of need to get a hold of Keara for longer then ten minutes." I stated while running a nervous hand through my hair, I had never asked her for the phone. So I was hoping that the offer still stood.

"Ah yes, come on in, I'll get it for ya." she stated as she pushed the door open for me, I entered her dark abode. Someone had told me she was a witch, it was of course another neighbor who didn't fancy her, but I knew she wasn't. Becka just liked the occult and thought of herself as a fortune teller, she had tried it on me with tarot cards, she told me that I had a dark past and a bright future . . . well one thing was right at least. Her apartment was dark and smelled strongly of sandalwood incense. Escaping to her bedroom she soon came back out with her phone, handing it to me, she again explained to me how too use it. When I first told her I had never used one she had laughed; now she just smiled.

"So, is it private? Cause you can take it back to your apartment if you'd like." she gave a wink and a little jab at my stomach,

I laughed. "Well sort of, and thanks again Becka, I owe ya." I told her, and gave her a large smile, she shook her head.

"Yea yea, just come true with that if this girls not the right one." again she winked and ushered me out of her apartment, she was an odd one, I never understood what she was talking about.

The phone rang a couple of times, and then Keara's voice came over the device.
"Ello?" she asked

"Hey, it's me, I got my neighbors phone we need to talk."

"Oh Fang, hey, I got great news I'll be out there in about two days, my publisher finally called me back, I'm getting my story done."

Her joy made me smile, I knew she loved to write, and did a good job on it, she had sent me some of her short stories . . . of course they were hard to read but I managed through a lot of them.

"That's great luv, but I got some strange things going on." I quickly and in detail told her of Black Mist's visit, I left out the voice in the woods only leaving that as my own foolish imagination. She listened to it intently only interrupting to ask me questions on different people and places.

"So . . . Kofra wants to kill everyone?" she asked

JOURNEY THROUGH THE DARK WOODS | 69

"Um, I don't think its that simple, but something like that, I have no idea what she is gonna do, but its something big if Black Mist is involving Tara, he loves her, he wouldn't endanger her life for something stupid." the words flowed out pretty fast, it was amazing to think that I still thought any good of him, even after he had abandoned me to stay with the pack.

"Ok, well maybe I can try to get out there tomorrow. It sounds like we have a lot to work on, oh Fang; I wish this would have been more of a happier time." I hoped she was telling the truth, my breath caught up in my throat, my mind reeled with the idea that she might also share my feelings.

"Yea I know, listen Keara, after this is all over . . . what were you planning on doing? Did you want too stay in America with me? Or go back to England?" her voice was quite on the other end, she didn't reply for a couple of breaths.

"Well . . . I don't know yet, we'll see, I was thinking of staying with you . . . is there anyway you would come back to England?" I shook my head, but then quickly remembered that she couldn't see me.

"Sorry luv, but I don't think I can, maybe someday, or if we have to attack Kofra I'll be there and we'll see if those old memories do come back to haunt me." both of us fell silent for a second, soon Keara's voice rang in my ear.

"I'll be there tomorrow Fang. I've been working on my Magick and I think I can teleport myself there. Hopefully right to your apartment, I've got the address and everything and I've seen pictures of the place on-line, so it shouldn't be too hard . . . hopefully." Magick was not my forte, I couldn't work it well, I could barely read Aura's but I knew that she could do it and after assuring her of that she soon sounded relieved as well. After chatting for a couple more minutes we both agreed that at night would be better. Incase she did miscalculate and ended up outside so no one would be up too see her appear out of no where. We both said our goodbyes and I returned the phone to Becka with many thanks.

After talking with Keara it was now almost eight in the morning, I again showered and headed out for the day. I had house work to do at another lady's home, this woman though wasn't elderly she just had a broken leg. From word of mouth she had heard about how I did yard work and random chores for money and had sought me out by leaving a message at the apartment's main office phone. Upon coming too her house, I noticed that there was a smell of magick about it. This was odd indeed, seeing as I hadn't noticed any magick in this neighborhood. Knocking at her door, the thing opened and a middle aged woman stood there, her silvery hair was braided down her back, and her blue eyes were strong and kind, her smile was true but when she looked at me it faded.

"Are you . . . no you can't be?" She asked, her voice was light and airy, she stood upon crutches with a brace on her leg, but her arms shook slightly.

"I'm Cody." I let out, damn it! Did she know I was a werewolf; would I have to move after all?

"Oh . . . well come in young sir." she said, her eyes never leaving my face. I came in too her house, it was opened and spacious not like my cramped little living area.

"Lovely house ya got here ma'am." I told her, she smiled, as she told me about the different cleanings she needed done on the place, I set too work and at about noon she called me back in to the house after I was done cleaning her gutters.

"Cody, I need to ask you something, how old do I look?" she asked, as she poured me a cup of spiced tea, we were seated in her living room she had a tray of cookies set out as well.

"Um . . . Well . . . I'm not sure, over fifty?" I questioned, she seemed younger, but her silvered hair and crows feet at the corners of her eyes told me otherwise. She let out a light laugh.

"I get that a lot, I am actually thirty five, yes I know, fairly young. You see Cody, a human doesn't actually have the metabolism to handle magick it eats us away faster, aging us quicker." I let my jaw drop; she talked of magick as though it was a normal conversation.

"I . . . er, well this is interesting." she smiled at me as she sipped her tea; I followed her example letting the rich taste fall over my tongue and down my throat.

"I knew you were different Cody, when I first saw you, you have a darker Aura, and I know you have a soul . . . but what are you?" I swallowed dryly, I stared at her, she was so sweet looking, as though she shouldn't know any of the horrors that might spring from my lips.

"Well, Joyce . . ." She had introduced herself after I had started my chores. "I'm a werewolf." I let it out bluntly, her eyes widened a little; she took another sip and set her cup down.

"How interesting, may I ask you some questions, I have been so curious about Werewolves, but have never met one." again my jaw dropped, this lady whom had only wanted me around for random chores now wanted to know all about being a werewolf, of course not being rude, I allowed her too ask questions. She asked me almost everything there was too being a werewolf, and I answered her too the best of my knowledge and experience. After her questions, I finally piped in.

"Excuse me, but how did you learn about these things?"

She smiled, "Well you see, my mother was a witch . . . but sadly that gene was not passed to me, but I studied the magick she used anyways. Like I said before, humans can't handle magick like real magick users can. And yes, I know of the risks, it's just so fascinating I couldn't help myself." she smiled and took up her cup again and smelled the rich tea. I stared intently at her, she intrigued me, yet I knew I couldn't get close too her. Getting close to humans was bad . . . they died so easily, unlike me.

"I should go . . . I have things to do." I whispered, and thanked her; she also thanked me for my information, and wished me luck in the world.

As I went back to my apartment I realized nothing in this world was what it seemed, I hadn't noticed but Joyce's questions had continued until the sun was almost setting. I could sense it, almost like it was watching over me. Letting out a long sigh, I continued on too my home. Passing by the wooded trails again, a sharp smell brought my attention to the place. Blood, it was rich and thick, and filled my nostrils. Letting out a growl I took off on the trail, letting my strength carry my feet, I ran towards the smell. Erupting out of the foliage, I landed in a small clearing away from the criss-crossing trails. There yellow eyes met mine, its fur was ragged and brown and covered in mange. Its checks were sunken and blood dripped from its mouth, as it stood over the dead human at its feet. The human didn't even look like it had been a living thing, its body was covered in blood, intestines and worse things lay around the ground. The smell of the blood almost knocked me back.

"WHAT HAVE YOU DONE?" I bellowed at the miserable looking werewolf, whom had to be a Lobo, a tribe that was the scavengers and the low lives of the world. It bared its teeth at me, no human understanding lay beneath its eyes. It was rouge, one whom had spent so much time in its wolf form it had forgotten to be human. I felt the change before I even thought of it. The muscles and bones popped, as the beast tore itself from my human body. Strong and muscular, I knew I was formidable in wolf form, I was larger then any timber wolf in this human world and stronger then it too. My fur was black and my eyes were a dark yellow, I was a thing of nightmares. The Lobo was half my size and it knew it, but it, no definitely male, was hungry and wanted its kill. Snapping my teeth at it I let out a fierce guttural growl, the creature before me growled back. But it did something I wasn't expecting, it ran! The stupid creature ran towards the populated streets. I followed, I was luckily faster, and better fed, letting out a burst of energy, I leapt up and toppled the meager wolf beneath me. Letting out a painful yowl, my body weight brought him to the ground. Felling bones crunch under my paws, I pulled open my jaws and bit down, along the mongrels spine. Snap! The spine broke beneath my teeth, another howl of pain echoed out of his blooded jowls. Turning him over, I dug in too the soft under belly, its bloodied gurgling cries were soon softened when his open jaws found my shoulder and bit down, I let out a painful grunt, but pressed on. I had to kill him, he was attacking humans, and he didn't know what he was anymore! Just a mindless, soulless thing that would soon fall away and become something that every Werewolf feared, a Nameless One! An undead, unknowing leech of the world, killing and slaughtering for its own miserable pleasure. The Lobos jaws tightened on my shoulder, as I finally found its pulsating heart. Opening my jaws I bite down and pulled. Feeling the fluttering thing in my jaws, the salty blood spilled from my mouth as the heart finally stopped. The creature's jaws relaxed on my shoulder as I kicked it away. Shaking and triumphant, I shook the wet blood from my fur as best I could, focusing my mind, I let the beast slid back in too my human body. Bones popping and muscles moving the creature melted away, leaving me panting, naked and bloody in the woods.

I laughed bitterly, remembering the first time I had changed in front of Keara, it was an illusion to keep ones clothes on, and you had to keep your mind focused on it. It was an old magick trick that Tara had taught me, when she was sick of seeing both Black Mist and I naked after hunting parties. My anger had made me forget about that trick and now I had a serious problem on my hands. How did I get back to my Apartment without the cops being called on me? Sighing I straightened up and yelped in pain as the wound on my shoulder gushed a little more blood on being moved.

"Shit!" I breathed as I examined my shoulder. It was a bloody patch where all you could see was torn flesh and blood. It was still bleeding and wasn't healing, I had been told that a rouge usually carried diseases and could sometimes slow the healing process on a normal werewolf. Now I knew that was true, I could normally heal such wounds without much thought. As long as they weren't inflicted with silver or pure magick, then I was fine. Looking up at the starry night, I sighed, at least it was dark, this might be easier then it sounded. Running through the dark wooded area I followed it too my apartment complex, luckily it was fairly close too it. Smelling the air, I made sure no human life was around and sprinted towards the apartments. Making it up the stairs and in too my apartment I closed the door and slid to the linoleum flooring. The wounds' bleeding was slowing, but I had lost too much blood. My hands were almost white and my legs were weak. I crawled to my bath room and managed to wrap a towel around my shoulder and found a pair of sweat pants to cover up my nakedness. Lying down on my bed, my eyes flickered and soon sleep took hold of my painful mind.

4

Dreams

*"T*HOMAS!*" I YELLED furiously as I pushed and moved through the throbbing bodies around me, the mob was in large numbers, but I had a wolf's strength on my side. My brother stood upon a large pedestal, his hair was darker then mine and his eyes were a rich hazel, most people mistook us as twins. I reached too him, the fear of loosing him again washed over my mind. I had watched him from the shadows, as I had become a demon and couldn't bare too let him see me. When he caught sight of me, he only smiled, but it didn't reach his eyes. As though he knew he would die, and that for some odd and twisted reason, everything was going too be alright. Another cry escaped my lips, yet no one heard me, as the hangman stalked over too him, his dark robes surrounded him in a shadowy void. The hood turned too me and only glowing red eyes stared out. No one else in the crowd seemed to notice that, they all just cheered and yelled, as I tried to push past them . . . why wasn't I getting closer? Why couldn't I make it? The people held me back! The hangman came behind my brother and pushed him off, the rope became taught as Thomas's neck snapped instantly. There would be no show for the people this time. An animalistic cry erupted from my trembling lips as I feel back in too the crowd. Letting them carry me back to the dark area of my life. Soon darkness engulfed me and I was falling. I didn't know why and I didn't care, Thomas was dead . . . and I couldn't save him. Not even with my new found strength or powers. I was still useless to the world . . .*

"Oh Silver Fang, look what I have for you." a dark and cold voice whispered in my ear, I felt nothing, as a whip lined in silver etched itself in too my back, I had done wrong

and I was being punished for it. I knew the voice; it was Juniper, her catlike physique stood in front of me.

"Yes, its true Silver Fang, I do much worse then torture my victims. I give them back something that they have lost!" she purred as her clawed hand began too glow with an iridescent light, she stabbed it in too my chest. I gagged and coughed, as a burning crept through my body. Then in a wave, everything I had ever done, all of the tortures I had been part of, every horrible memory came rushing back in too my memory. I could see every persons face clearly inside of my mind as I killed them or maimed them.

"NO!" I screamed, tears streaming down my face.

"Oh yes, I give you back your soul." she whispered in too my ear . . .

I was alone again, sitting in the dark, a door opened behind me, and my father staggered in. he was taller bulkier then myself. I had gotten my mothers looks, while Thomas had taken after Him.

"You little ingrate! Crying and whining!" he screamed at me, I had remembered it all. He was a drunk after my mother died. He would beat me and go away for weeks on end drinking with his 'friends'.

"No, I didn't do anything." I whispered my voice was light, like a child's. I looked down, I was fifteen again and not strong enough to fight off my father's wrath. He raised his arm and swung at me, I took the blow falling back on too the ground.

"YOU WERE THE REASON SHE DIED! YOU TOOK HER AWAY!!! I SHOULD HAVE KILLED YOU AS SOON AS HER WOMB SPAT YOU OUT! YOU FUCKING BASTARD!" his words seared in too my mind as I flailed wildly to try and shield myself from his blows. Blood trickled from the scratch along my eye and from my lip which was already swelling.

"NO I DIDN'T!!!" I yelled back, as I shoved him away from me . . .

I feel again in too the darkness, my mind couldn't hold on too all of these memories . . . Where was I?

"FANG! Wake up!" a frightened voice shouted above me, as I swung wildly, trying to get the attacker away from me. Something pulled at my shoulder which sent a sharp pain, like fire, through my mind. I swung again and my hand met flesh. Something fell away from me.

"Please wake up! You're having a nightmare!" it was a girls voice, someone who I knew . . . but who? I opened my eyes for the first time, a thin band of light came through the closed blinds in my bedroom, and a face was above me. It was the most beautiful face I had ever seen. Her hair was a rich auburn, but her bangs were yellow like a flame. Her chocolaty eyes stared down at me; a bruise was forming on her perfect untouched face. "Keara?" I asked, my voice a shaky tremor from my lips. She smiled, oh that smile! It could light a thousand worlds, even with that look, my eyesight clouded and I was again in the world of darkness.

Opening my eyes again, there was no sunlight coming through my blinds, just darkness. Something smelled good, like a mixture of chicken and vegetables, sniffing again I realized there were also herbs involved. Straightening up in my bed, my shoulder protested. For the first time sense I had been unconscious, I looked at my wound. It had a large gauze bandage on it, and didn't hurt as much as it had last night . . . last night? Keara? It all flooded back to me. She had been here, I hadn't dreamt that . . . but was I the one who had marred her perfect face?

"Keara?" I asked the darkness of my room, I heard footsteps in the kitchen, pushing myself off the bed; I wobbled to the door, my balance slowly returning to me. Keeping my hand on the wall, I made it out of the cave that was my room. Opening the door and allowing my eyes to adjust to the new light, I surveyed the kitchen. She stood with her back turned to me, her hair was shorter then it had been in the Darkwoods, it was now just too her shoulders. She stood almost a head shorter then me, and her frame was petite but well muscled, not bony or skinny. Wearing a short sleeved white blouse, I noticed that she was also clad in a sage green peasant skirt. I had never seen her in a skirt before, my lips twitched from a smile.

"Keara?" I asked again, my voice was a fine tremble; she turned suddenly, her smile large on her face, but so was the bruise from my fist on the left side of her cheek.

"Fang, oh thank God! I thought you were going to sleep for a week." her voice was pleasant to hear, like chimes on a light wind.

"Oh . . . did I?" I asked stupidly as I pointed to her cheek. Putting a graceful hand up to her smooth skin she touched it lightly.

"It's alright; you were having a nightmare when I got here, probably from that nasty infection. I was trying to wake you, but I forgot something important. You're strong; you could easily smash a person's skull in. I should of let you just sleep it off." she smiled again and came closer to me, and simply put her arms around me and buried her face in too my chest. I tensed slightly, and hugged her back.

"Oh luv . . . I'm sorry I did that. It was a crazy dream . . . How did you get here so fast?" I asked, she pulled away, and walked back to her cooking, I had been right it looked like a mixture of chicken and vegetables, that she was stir frying.

"Well, when you told me about Black Mist, I decided to come out sooner. But I left early; something was bothering me . . . as though I knew you were sick. And when I got here you were lying in your room, fast out and still bleeding from that wound you got. So, I used what little healing magick I knew to get the infection out and ran to the store to get supplies. You really need to keep your refrigerator stocked, it was totally empty when I got here." she laughed at that, and I couldn't help it, I let out a laugh as well. Pulling out two plates from the cabinet she dished up the food. Smelling the rich scents, my stomach growled hungrily, I had no idea of how long I had been out. Digging in like a starving man, I ate most of the food, while Keara slowly picked at her small plate.

"Well, Fang, you really need to tell me how you got that nasty bite wound. And what were you dreaming about? You were yelling all sorts of things, like Thomas, and something about your soul?" I swallowed the last bite of food and stared deeply at her, she was of course serious she wanted to know.

"Herm, ok, I'll tell you." I quickly told her of the rouge Lobo whom had taken the humans life in the woods, and how it had gotten a hold of my shoulder. She listened quietly, but when I didn't tell her about my dreams she pressed on.

"You remember, I told you Thomas was my brother, he was killed by an angry mob. They thought he was different. He always knew about strange things and it made the town folk really scared of him. I couldn't save him, he was hung . . . my dream was making me relive it again. Then I was with Juniper. It was when she caught me and cursed me in too the Darkwoods. She used a whip lined in silver for one of my tortures." I turned slightly to Keara to show her the angry scars lining my back, one of Junipers favorite things to put on prisoners. She surveyed them, and had me press on with the story. "But that was a cake walk to what she then put on me . . . she gave me back my soul . . . don't look surprised, I had my soul for a bit as a young werewolf. But as I started to kill and fall deeper within the Daligulven pack, I lost it . . . she returned it and with that all of the pain I had inflicted on people came back to me and ate at me. Guilt is one thing you don't feel when you don't have a soul . . ." I sighed, trying to bring back the next memory that came with my dreams. I had never really told Keara about my parents . . . she just simply watched me, so intrigued with the story that her food lay untouched in front of her. "My father was the last dream . . . after my mother died; he began to drink and to get violent. He would beat me, and scream and yell at my brother." I touched the scar on my eyebrow. "That's how I got this. He gave it too me . . . he was beating me again when you woke me up. That's probably why I was swinging so violently . . . and I am so sorry about that bruise." I stared down at my feet, not wanting to see any accusation in her eyes. I felt a hand on my working shoulder. Looking up, Keara was standing by me, light tears traced her eyes.

"Fang, I didn't know. I'm so sorry about all of those dreams. If I could I would take them all away for you." She knelt besides me so that our eyes could meet.

"I don't care what you did in the past. It's who you are now, that's the person who's my friend, not the person you were long ago. Way before I was even born." her smile made my heart skip a few beats.

After discussing my dreams and my wound, Keara got down to business on telling me what she had found out about the Daligulven pack and Kofra's plan. Apparently the news of her thinking up stuff had been traveling around the inner circles of high magicks.

"It's odd really; she's been getting different books, all having to deal with Ritual and Blood Magicks." Keara continued I shivered at the idea of Blood Magicks that was nasty stuff to get mixed up in. "And different artifacts from the time of the Great

War between the werewolves." The Great War was indeed a war to end all wars, it lasted fifty years, at least that's what I was told, it was between the Faolon's (their supporting tribes) and the Tala's (and their supporting tribes), no one really told me what it was over, but it was a large turning point in Were civilization. "So, it appears she is trying to cast a very direct spell, something to do with old magicks that haven't been used for centuries. Is Kofra a good magick user?" I grimaced at her question; Kofra had been one of the cruelest magick users I had ever met. She never used traditional forms of magick but went in too the dark and arcane forms.

"Let's just say she's been studying dark magicks for over a thousand years, I think she has a leg up on us." I simply put it, I couldn't bring myself too tell Keara the evil things that Kofra had done to anyone who disobeyed her. The images of decapitations and tortures more gruesome then any living creature could tolerate flashed in my mind. I shivered with the memories, which made Keara raise her eye brows.

"That bad?" she asked, I nodded, taking in a deep breath of air, I forced a smile.

"Something's I'd like to forget . . . anyway, we really need to figure out what she is up too. When can we get investigating? Can you get any help from the Earth Guardian Council?" the Earth Guardian Council was, of course, formed of only Earth Guardians, there were about two for each continent, and Juniper, whom pretty much over saw them. Keara shook her head; she also forced a smile while her shoulders slumped a little, as though she was defeated, her brow wrinkled in thought.

"Sadly I am a rookie among them. They don't take much stock in anything I say or come up with. So my word means little too them. Maybe in a couple more decades? But I don't think we have that sort of time now do we. And I have no idea how long it will take you're shoulder too heal, it could be unusable for a couple of days." I frowned, not being able too help for a couple of days? Did we have that long? I voiced my questions to Keara, she figured we could head off tomorrow. We would be going to meet up with a very old magick user, someone who made me look like a young pup.

"Well, this should be interesting." I mumbled, Keara only smiled and with that simple gleam of hope coming from her. I knew we could do this, my heart and my mind told me we could. With her brain and my strength, we might overcome this stupid obstacle . . . and then I could see if she cared for me . . . the way I cared for her.

Sleeping arrangements were simple, Keara forced me to take the bed, seeing as I was 'injured' even though I had sustained worse in my days of villainy. She refused and of course being a woman, got her way. I did take the bed, but it was a small area and could really only fit one body and my frame was too big to squeeze in another person. So, she took the floor, removing the cushions from my hand me down couch she made herself up a bed. Explaining that she had slept on worse, I only pouted at her, acting like an ignorant child seemed to make her laugh and that was always a good noise. After the moon took over the night sky, Keara lay peacefully on her make shift bed. Her hair fanned out around her head, making a halo of fire. I sighed, the sweet smell of her scent had made it hard to sleep in the Darkwoods, and it still had the same affect on me. Poking her gently with my foot, she simple turned over and paid me no mind. Smiling too myself, I slowly and carefully got off my little bed, without making a sound, I laid down gently besides her, trying not to wake her. She again stirred in her sleep, making me pause, but she soon settled. Lying down besides her, I put my arm around her, which didn't seem to make her move. After a little while, she snuggled up to me, as though in her subconscious she knew I was there. Letting out a gentle sigh, I soon found myself asleep.

5

Green Eyes

REACHING OUT OF a foggy dreamland I found myself lying by Keara. It had not been a dream, she was with me. Her soft scent of lavender and basil filled my nostrils. It was strange how females always smelled of natural herbs or flowers, while males seemed to just have a musky or spicy smell about them. Smiling too myself, I slowly got up, not allowing her too even feel me move away from her, escaping the darkness of my room. The microwave only read five a.m., and that was sleeping in for me. Most Were's tended to only need to sleep for about five hours. But because of my injury the need for sleep took over me for healing I found myself with at least eight hours of sleep under my belt. Stretching stiffly in my cramped kitchen, my shoulder pulled and a trickle of pain ran down my arm. Gritting my teeth, I pulled the bandage off of my shoulder all of the way. The wound was already half healed; a fresh scab was laced over the main part of the bite. Though I knew that if I stretched too hard or did something stupid it would tare open. Rummaging around in my cupboards I pulled out my 'welcome to the neighborhood' gift, a coffee maker, I had only used the thing once. And that had taken Becka's help, seeing as my skills with new technology were lack luster. Automatically my dislike for coffee had grown, the stuff was disgusting and bitter but I knew that Keara drank it and would love to have a cup of it. Following the steps on the contraption I finally got the coffee to start to brew. Luckily my reading skills were good enough for me too follow directions on things, or my life wouldn't work very smoothly in this world. A yawn came from my room, I smiled, one good thing about being a werewolf, I

79

could hear everything if I wanted too, especially in this little apartment. Keara soon shuffled out of the bedroom her hair meshed up, and sleep still in her eyes and the bruise on her cheek fully healed and gone. Another yawn escaped her lips as she knuckled her eyes, and still in that rumpled sleepy stage, I knew her beauty was something no other woman could surpass.

"Oh 'ello Fang, did you sleep well . . . wow . . . your wound, I didn't think it would be that healed." she exclaimed, stepping up closer to me too examine the wound. Her fingers trailed along the edges of it, sending a shiver through me. Luckily she didn't seem to notice.

"This is amazing, well good things are bound to happen . . . are you making coffee?" her eyes grew larger and brighter, as though just the word she spoke could caffeinate her. "Why yes, I am, see I can totally do this real world stuff." my grin was spreading across my face faster then I thought it would. Soon she was drinking the bitter stuff, and I was off to shower. After fighting a diseased werewolf and then not showering for three days, I was sure I didn't have the greatest aroma about me. The hot water burned when it hit my shoulder but I ignored the pain. I had endured much worse then this and too be clean was a glorious thing. Exiting the still steaming bathroom, Keara had made short work of the pot of coffee. She took over my bathroom while I fetched different clothes to wear. And then decided to pack a small bag for 'traveling'. even though I knew I would be fine in one set of clothes, but, if I had another run in with a creature that really got me infuriated I couldn't risk running around naked for the rest of our travels. I was sure Keara would agree with this, she didn't seem like the sort of girl who wasn't fazed by nudity. Soon Keara was also out of the shower, her scent was diluted with soaps but I could still smell her sweetness under it all.

"So, I think we can head out soon. I have an idea of getting some information. The magick user I mentioned before is an Oracle, I researched her before coming over here." she told me of the plan, and we decided to hop the trains. But first we had too head too the major city of Portland too do that, Taxi's were a nice thing, seeing as I didn't have a drivers license or a car. All of it was fairly cheap, even though I had pretty much sold off my gold and silver coins for mortal money. I still had enough for two tickets to the next county.

The train itself was large and wobbled while it speed over the tracks. When I had first seen a train it had scared me, but I knew they were safe . . . mainly because Keara had told me this.

"So, Fang, how is life working out for you? You know doing odd jobs and all?" she asked trying to make polite conversation over the train ride. I let out a sigh

"Well, it was working alright I had enough for rent and bills, and I liked working with people too try and get myself used to them again." I put in; Keara had never understood what it was like for me being around people. When you're an animal, and you haven't been around humans, they only smell like food, their fears their adrenaline, made the beast inside of me rear its ugly head. But after living around them again, I soon could control those impulses to hunt and kill better. She nodded her head, as though she knew what I was thinking. Could she read me better then I thought? It was hard too know with her, her magick could read my aura better then I could read people's body languages.

"I can sort of imagine, I was alone most of the time . . . but I never had your . . . um . . . desires?" she tried to make my beast sound like a normal conversation, for if anyone was listening to us, it would sound like I had some sort of vise I was getting over. "Yea . . . it's really different. I couldn't imagine you going through it. You would make a weird one." I joked, though Keara's eyes seemed worried, as though she was thinking of something far off and I couldn't read them.

"Hey, Luv? Are you okay?" I asked her, my voice seemed to bring her back to the present.

"No its fine, I was just thinking . . . what are you going to do after this?" my mind railed with the ideas, my mind wanted me too simply say, I would live with you, but my lips and tongue didn't want to move. I didn't know how to respond, so I made something up. "Um . . . well I am not sure, I guess I could figure it out when it comes around . . . I'm sure your just gonna go on with your stories and stuff." stupid, stupid! That wasn't a good answer, Keara chewed on her bottom lip, was she as nervous as me, her scent didn't change and her heart beat stayed about the same. Whatever she was thinking must have been more internal then I could read.

"Well, I guess that's what I was planning. I like writing my stories . . . but apparently with being an Earth Guardian I get a payment so I can live comfortably. It's about five thousand a week." my jaw dropped, the idea of thousands of dollars for just one week! "Well . . . wow . . . damn Keara that's a lot of money, what are you gonna do with it all?" I leaned forward in my chair; they were right across from each other with our little bags under the seats. We both hadn't taken much.

"Um . . . I was thinking of buying a house, and petitioning to live in America . . ." she trailed off; I stared at her, that's all I could do, while my jaw was hanging slightly open. I probably looked like a putz but I really didn't care. She was thinking of living in America? To be with me? I could only imagine, she had grown up in England and loved it there.

"You mean switch with the American Earth Guardian?" I asked stupidly, I knew the answer; I just wanted her to explain more.

"Yea, they have my petition from the last Earth Guardian meeting . . . they are thinking about it. But the American Earth Guardian wants a new location so I think it will work." she swallowed hard, I could hear it, I wanted to smile, I wanted to hug her. But I wasn't sure she was doing this for me? How could I? I had never asked her how she felt about me.

"And I figured . . . well . . . maybe, you could, you know just stay with me? I would get a house with a basement. So that on the full moons I could watch over you?" her voice grew smaller, her scent gave off uncertainty I smiled.

"Yea, that sounds great." it was great, I would be with her . . . but what if she only wanted me there to keep me away from the public . . . did she think I was dangerous . . . damn it! Shut up! She wants you too stay with her! I sealed my worries in the back of my mind for later. "So . . . not changing subject on purpose . . . but how did you find out about this Oracle?" Keara sagged down slightly in her chair; she seemed relived to go off topic.

"Actually I heard of her from the other Earth Guardians they say she's really good. Apparently she channels Essence. That's a human's memories trapped in a spirit like form, and she gets her knowledge from them. I am sort of excited to see what she does." Her excitement did radiate though her, her eyes started to sparkle again, and her voice was upbeat. I smiled, and agreed; magick had also always brought an interest in me, though not as much as Keara, I didn't know enough about the mystical arts for me to be bouncing around in my seat. Soon the train stopped and we got off, bustling through the large terminal that was crammed packed with people, it was almost hard to breathe with out smelling everyone's sweaty unwashed body. My stomach jarred a little, then I finally got out in too the open air of the city streets, it started feeling better. Following Keara we made our way in a city I didn't know. Thank God for maps, because without the one she had we would have been lost.

The shop we ended up at was what Becka called 'a hippie place' there were tie-dyed sheets up on the wall and a Celtic depiction of the goddess as well. The person at this shop seemed to sell everything from incense to focusing crystals and tarot cards. The shop was small and tidy; a lazy black and white cat lay happily on the check stand. It opened a yellow eye at us and quickly got up and scuttled off to the back room which had hanging beads blocking it from the main shop. Keara raised an eyebrow and only continued to examine the items. Soon the cat came back and claimed its place on the top of the check stand again, and a lady also came out. She had a messy rumpled pony tail made up of dark blonde hair, with wisps of silver in it. Her eyes were large and brown, but were behind thin glasses, her face was longer and sharper, but over all she was pleasant and not ugly. She wore a short sleeved dark green tunic like dress that fell to her feet, with a black tie of satin around it.

"Yes, Hello, and welcome to my shop." her voice was matter of fact and straight forward. Keara spoke up, "Well, 'ello, we are in search of someone, maybe you can help us?" the strange woman's eyebrows went up high on her forehead and then she finally looked at me, and did a double take. Her eyes unfocused and came back at me. She stumbled back, almost falling over in too her displays, Keara and I stared at her dumbfounded.

She gasped, "You're a . . . a lycanthrope!" she said, pointing at me, I tried to smile, but she was afraid of me, thank God Keara was there or she would of died from a heart attack. "Yes, yes he is, but he is good, he wont hurt you . . . he's my friend. I'm an Earth Guardian and I need an oracle's help." The women straightened and stared at me harder.

"Well then . . . I guess I can trust the word of a Guardian . . . what do you need, I am happy too help."

Next thing I knew we were seated on large fluffy pillows that covered most of the backroom, the woman, whom had introduced herself as Catrice was the Oracle; she channeled the spirits and all of that. She sat across from us; she had taken off her glasses and had focusing crystals in front of her. Also a mixture of sharp smelling herbs were in a small wooden bowl, she took them and sprinkled them on her head.

"Now, I will be channeling Essence, it will be a spirit, generally from the past of one of you. I have no control over who comes and I can't tell you what they will give you. Some don't give much information, but others do . . . now, please, I need a drop of blood from both of you for this too work." she held out a small dagger, from the way the low lights gleamed off of it, it was polished silver and would be able to cut my skin. Keara held out her hand, Catrice pricked her finger, Keara flinched, but didn't complain, she let a drop fall in too the little bowl. I held me hand out, I felt the sharp pain of the prick but it was the burning sensation that followed that held more pain. Pure silver did burn the flesh of all Were's when it was cut in too them, my blood fell down in too the bowl as well. The wound was blackened around the edges but it would heal.

Catrice struck a match and threw it in too the bowl, it burnt and an awful smell perfumed from it. Pushing back a gag, I watched her eyes close. Something pulled at me, Keara gasped slightly, as the magick flooded out from the woman before us, the thin tendrils of magick glistened across my skin, raising a chill from me. The temperature dropped, a thin line of fog came from my lips, and from Keara's; she looked at me sideways and then looked back at Catrice. Her eyes were still closed . . . but she wasn't breathing, I couldn't hear her, and I couldn't see her chest rising and falling, I reached out a hand to her. But Keara grabbed my arm, her eyes were wide, she mouthed the word "Look" I obeyed. Catrice's eyes were no longer closed and no longer brown, but a rich emerald green that stared out at us.

"Cody . . . my boy . . ." Catrice's voice wasn't hers either . . .

"Oh God!" I whispered the voice was my mothers.

"Cody . . . you seek knowledge that will hopefully help you and your friend." she breathed in heavily, Keara stayed motionless by my side.

"Mother?" I asked, Keara took in a sharp breath of air, but I couldn't pull my eyes away from Catrice . . . who had taken the Essence of my Mother.

"Yes . . . I miss you, oh how you have grown; I wish I could have more time with you." Catrice's hand reached out and touched me lightly on the cheek, I couldn't move away from her. So I sat and watched.

"You look for the werewolf Kofra . . . she is in England, your friends are watching her closely . . . but she wishes to do something she did too you once . . . oh Cody . . . what she is planning." Tears welled up in her eyes, I could feel my own eyes water as well, but I blinked them back.

"The items she has gathered will allow her to command a spell of great power . . . it will help her to take the souls of every living creature on this planet . . . please . . . stop her. With the love you both share you can defeat her . . . but be weary Cody, this will be a hard trial for you." I stared at her, my mind railed with what she had told me, Kofra, taking the souls of the people on this plain? How could she do it, it would case everyone to feel no guilt and commit cruelties that they have never imagined.

"I . . . mum . . . was it you . . . was it you talking to me in the woods?" I asked, before I could even ask more about Kofra, I had to know if it was her voice, it had remained genderless . . . but I had to know.

"No . . . it wasn't me . . . I am sorry Cody, someone else whom loves you is watching you as well. Please be careful . . . I lo . . ." Catrice took a large shaky breath, and closed her eyes. She then had her normal brown eyes, she looked confused.

"Did everything go okay?" she asked, my eyes had watered up, everything was a blur, my mind raced, and I had to get out of there. Before I even thought it I felt my body move. I jumped up and ran out of that place; I could hear Keara yell my name. But my mind was too scared. My mother was the spirit she called, why! Why her? Why couldn't she of gotten someone else. I could barely even remember her; she died when I was so young, of a sickness that I still had no name for. It was hard watching her drift away before my eyes, now I had to be reminded of her, after a thousand years, I was still that five year old boy . . . crying over his mother. I stopped outside of the shop, and saw a shaded alley by it; I ran in too in, punching my fists against the brick walls that surrounded me helped the emotions that troubled me so. Fist sized holes stared back at me, looking at them, I knew that I could easily rip down this building in a rage . . .

"Fang?" I light voice asked behind me. It was Keara, I felt calmer, as though her very presence made me aware of what I was doing.

"Fang . . . I'm so sorry." she whispered, she put a hand lightly on my working shoulder. Taking in a long shaky breath, I turned to her.

"Why her?" I whispered and dropped to my knees, I reseeded back in too my mind, the tears came out before I could even try to stop them. Keara wrapped her arms around me; I shook with the sobs that escaped me.

"Fang, please, stop, I am so sorry about this, it's all my fault." she whispered, I stopped, and took her face in my hands; her eyes were wide and rimmed with tears.

"It will never be your fault!" I told her, I slowly let go of her face, she kept kneeling by me. Breathing lightly, she stood up slowly, looking up, I forced a smile.

"No, Keara, I am sorry about what I did. I couldn't stay in there, it was just hard. She died when I was five, I barely remember her, but she was the only parent I had that made sense to me. She actually loved me . . . my father just kept us as property." I stood up, and met her eyes; they were still wide with light tears.

"I guess we really need to stop Kofra . . ." I offered Keara nodded.

JOURNEY THROUGH THE DARK WOODS

"Yea, from what your mother said, what Kofra is planning . . . oh God, that would make life a living hell." putting the haunting eyes of my Mother out of my mind, we went back in too the shop, to explain a little of what happened to Catrice. Keara was kind enough not too tell her it was my Mother, but just an interesting person from my past whom brought back mixed feelings. Catrice bid us good luck and we took our leave.

Finally we found ourselves on another train, bound for the airport, Keara was too drained to teleport us and she still had a free round trip ticket from her publishers. I on the other hand had to buy one. Luckily it wasn't too much. On the plane ride, I clutched the seat as we took off Keara giggled lightly at me. My reactions too things always seemed to make her laugh. But soon we were in the air and I was staring out my window. Wondering what would happen if we fell? Bad thoughts, but I think I would live, so would Keara, she healed about as well as I did. As the plane went through the cloud layers I found myself falling asleep on the ten hour flight.

6

Returning Memories

UPON ARRIVING IN England my heart was racing from the landing. Getting out in too the over cast day of this land; we found a taxi and headed to Keara's flat. Starring out at the town houses that lined the winding road made my heart sink in too my stomach. This used too be my home, last I saw this place, was in the sixteenth century, when townhouses weren't around and the rich reined above the lower life. Brothels and gambling houses were the places I stalked and killed in, I never prayed upon the rich . . . it got too messy. But now with so many new buildings and complex's there was nothing left of the England I had once known.

"We're here." Keara's soft voice brought me back to the present. We were outside of a small apartment type complex, there were only about five flats in the whole building and Keara's was on the top floor.

Her flat was neat and tidy; there wasn't much furniture a love seat and a coffee table were in the middle of the living room. Large book shelves covered the whole wall, books of all sizes lining the shelves, and on the other side was one large window and by it was a flower painting. The kitchen was also small and neat, and the bathroom was across the hallway. Her bedroom was at the end of it, I smiled too myself, it was just like her, so organized.

"Well this is it. I guess we need to figure out the steps of our master plan." she raised an eyebrow at me and smiled; I nodded and sat down on the couch.

JOURNEY THROUGH THE DARK WOODS

"Do you want something to eat." just saying the word 'eat' made my stomach growl, I had only eaten a small meal on the plane.

"Yea that would be great, I am starving." Getting up I helped her in the kitchen and amazed her with making a very large sandwich. After eating almost all of the contents of Keara's refrigerator we sat down on the couch.

"Well, I have one way of getting hold of Tara, but I haven't done it for about twenty years." Keara looked interested, as I attempted to explain the very odd magickal process that I didn't even understand.

"Well, Tara, Black Mist and I were all linked magickally, we could communicate too each other with this connection. It's quite an interesting thing . . . but I haven't been able to connect to her for twenty years . . . it's like she has been blocking me." I shrugged and leaned back in too the couch, Keara looked a little confused.

"That is interesting, I've heard of that before, but the people who do it really have to know each other and trust or love one another." she pointed out, I smiled, we did love each other, Tara was like the sister I had never had and I would of trusted Black Mist with my life. I told Keara of these feelings,

"But it's been awhile sense I've seen Tara, she used to bring me new clothing and different things to the Darkwoods for me, when I was locked away."

She laughed. "That explains how you got those nice clothes there, I just thought you were lucky, but it makes sense now." I nodded, and told her I would set up a meeting place with Tara.

"Now, I am gonna um . . . 'zone' out and it would also help if you didn't touch me at anytime, or the connection will be lost." she agreed and stepped away from me, watching me from the kitchen. I reseeded in too my mind, and pulled on the tendrils of magick that linked me too Tara. A small voice sounded in my head.

"Cody?" she asked, her voice was small and unsure.

"Yea it's me girl, I'm in England, Keara and I are gonna help ya on the Kofra deal."

She sounded relieved. "Oh good, we need it, Black Mist has told me a plan, but I want too meet up with you."

"I was hoping you would say that, this is where we are." I projected the image of Keara's flat to Tara, she laughed.

"Okay, I know where that is, so it all works out, I'll be there tonight I really can't leave now . . . they're watching the woods closely, I can only move around at night. I have too go!" she cut off, I was snapped back in too the present world.

"Did you talk too her?" Keara asked she was still standing in the kitchen, her eyes wide. "Yea, I did, she's coming here tonight, so we just need to stay put. You have wards on this place right?" Wards were magickal locks and barriers on a house or object that you don't want certain people to get in too. It's even better then mundane locks. They also would help too shield the house of any magickal happenings inside and outside of the perimeter.

"Of course I do, I am an Earth Guardian, if I didn't anyone magickally sensitive would feel me here." she smiled and came back too sit with me on the couch.

After looking through most of her books on magick (a lot of which were in languages I didn't speak or were books of translated dead languages) we mainly sat and talked. When we had gotten in too London it was after one and we had a long time too wait for night too take place. I knew Tara; she would leave as soon as the moon rose to a certain point in the sky, which would be about eight or nine at night. It was strange being alone with Keara and not moving around, when I had first met her we walked the whole time with each other, I was an active person. I didn't like sitting around.

"What do you want to do Fang? You look like your ready too jump out of a window if we dally for any longer." she asked, jabbing me in the side a little so I would pay attention too her, my mind was on the outside world . . . in a place I hadn't been for over three hundred years. "Um, can you show me around your neighborhood a little?" I asked my tongue licking my dried lips, I wanted too see the city, I had to know what had taken place here and what was different. Keara agreed and we set out for the afternoon in the city, it was bustling with people trying to get to their destinations and no one even seemed to notice us. Keara lived on a road called Dunoon that was lined with houses and town houses, we made our way out of their and got to Forest Hill Road. It was still an over cast day but even though I was in the place where my family had all died and my first true love was slain, I was strangely happy. Everything had changed so much that it didn't even feel like the London I grew up in. after a good mile or so up the road, we reached Peckham Rye Park, it was a lovely spacious little park where we decided to walk around in. it reminded me a lot of the wooded area near the apartments I lived at. Keara was delighted with walking as well, the wind pushed her hair away from her shoulders and she was all smiles.

"So I must know why did you cut your hair? It was at your waist last I saw It." glancing up at me, Keara smiled again it reached her eyes, which made them sparkle.

"Well, I've always had long hair, and I decided to try something different. Do you like it?" her question was timid as though I might refute her, but I smiled back at her.

"I do, its nice, a lot easier too take care of too I can imagine." I had only had long hair once, and that was when I had been human, when I had turned I rebelled and cut it. It was the style then so no one cared if men had long hair. And it seemed like no one cared now either, men had all different styles of hair it seemed, same with women. Times had definitely changed, we passed a group of rough looking teenagers, and all of them had cigarettes hanging out of their mouths. And ridiculously tight clothing on, the only female of the party had a Mohawk that was dyed hot pink, I wanted too laugh. But Keara made us hurry by them.

"What was that? I have never seen kids look like that!" I said while I laughed heartily at them, Keara gave me a funny look and shook her head.

JOURNEY THROUGH THE DARK WOODS | 89

"Their punks that's what they are, there are more of them nowadays then there used too be. A lot of muggings happen in this park because of them." she scolded, giving a fierce look, I tried too plead innocent on not knowing what these punks were capable of, but I still ended up laughing.

"Oh luv they look like angry teenagers, they can't all be bad." Keara gave up and I didn't push the issue any farther. We finally decided too head back too her little flat and await Tara's arrival, for by the time we got back it was close to six in the evening. Keara and I swung by a food market on the way there and picked up dinner. As Keara made clear, she did not want a hungry werewolf as an ally in a fight. I agreed and we bought enough food too last a couple of meals.

"Why is it that you eat so much anyway?" she finally asked, as she chopped up vegetables in the kitchen while I again stared at her vast books.

"It's a werewolf thing, we just burn more energy then normal people, our heart beats and temperatures alone are higher then a human's, so we need to eat more too keep us going. You should see a group of werewolves eat, it's quite an interesting experience. You are libel to loose a hand." Keara laughed, but I hadn't intended it too be a joke. But she didn't need to know that, she prepared a large batch of spaghetti, with mushrooms and large chunks of onions and bell peppers that oozed through the sauce. It was absolutely delicious; I had no prior cooking knowledge and could barely make a thing of top ramen without it exploding on me. So I gave her what props she deserved and quickly devoured the food. By the time we were done cleaning up after dinner it was past eight, I felt a pull at my mind and a small voice speak in my ear.

"I'm coming." Tara whispered in too me, I could feel her emotions; she was overjoyed at being able to see me again. I showed her I was happy too and she cut off the connection. It still confused me as too why she disappeared for twenty years but I know I would hear that story another time, we had more interesting things at hand. Apparently I had a zoned out look on my face, for Keara finally waved a hand in front of me making me jump a little.

"You there?" she asked, her eye brows raised.

"Yea, Tara is on her way." Keara seemed happy with that answer, so we waited for the arrival of my oldest friend.

A knock sounded on the door a half hour later, Keara went too open it, and before she could even say hello Tara came through the door and shut it quickly behind her.

"Oh thank God you have wards!" she said loudly, her voice was a rich alto, with no accent on it. She had covered it up before she joined the pack apparently. Her hair was a rusty red color that fell past her shoulders in lazy curls that framed her heart shaped face. Her eyes were a dark knowledgeable brown that seemed to search a person harder then they knew. She shook her head and quickly turned it too me, she was wearing a pair of dirty jeans and a fairly tattered tank top, that barely covered her chest, she had a slimmer build but with muscles and curves that could knock a man flat.

"CODY!" she finally yelled and before I could even say anything back at her, she had pounced upon me, hugging me fiercely and planting a kiss upon my lips I blushed a little. I had at one time had romantic feelings toward Tara, but after a very awkward night and her realizing she was in love with Black Mist, she was, after all of that, then my sister. Keara coughed loudly to get our attentions, Tara quickly let go of me while I stood their dumbfounded.

"You must be Keara. Man is it good to be in a normal house, it sucks being in the woods." she smiled and went over and extended her hand to Keara who took it thoughtfully. Tara stood a good two inches taller then Keara, and then I finally noticed that Tara had no shoes on.

"Hey girl, what happened to your clothes?" I asked her, she sighed and rolled her eyes. "Its hard to keep clothes nice and pretty when you're crawling around in the dirt trying to find an easy access in to a fortress for two friends. Oh and Keara you are now my friend, any friend of Cody's is a friend of mine." she smiled broadly,

"Well thanks . . . I guess? Before you tell us this plan of yours, would you like to take a shower, and I have some clothes you could probably fit in too?" Keara offered, Tara's smile got bigger, if that was possible, and it seemed to make her look more feline.

"That would be lovely, show the way." Keara showed Tara the bathroom and found her some clothes. After that Keara came back out in too the Living room.

"She seems nice. What is she anyway?" she asked, I sat back down on the couch.

"Tara is a Kahn, she's a good magick user, and has a knack for making trouble, but she is a sweet person." I said, reclining backwards and stretching my arms in too the air.

"She seems it, so I take it you are close?" she asked, raising a questioning eyebrow at me and sitting down next to me.

"Yea, I had never had a sister until I met her. She's a good one too have." Keara seemed to relax, had she been jealous because she had kissed me? Those were questions I would have to ask her at another date. After waiting another ten minutes for Tara, she soon emerged clean and changed out of the bathroom.

"Oi that was amazing! I love being clean, okay kiddies you ready for the master plan?" she sat down on the edge of the coffee table in front of us. We both nodded.

"Well, there's no easy way in, Kofra is pretty good at keeping people out and in. tomorrow night, Black Mist is going too distract and get rid of the two Red Dragons in the front of the mansion." my breath caught in my throat, Tara didn't seem to notice or didn't react and kept talking. "I am gonna be working up a spell to lower Kofra's wards, you two are gonna slip in and execute the bitch and then we are off to the pub!

Easy eh?" she asked. All in all, it sounded easy, but with Tara, she tended too make things sound simpler then they were. Keara spoke up before I could react.

"Where is the Daligulven's fortress?" Tara's eyes sparkled a little bit,

"Well, it's outside of Barnet and Totterridge."

Keara almost laughed. "You can't be serious, they're that close to my home and I have never caught wind of them?" The Sparkle in Tara's eyes left, she began to become serious.

"Kofra is a powerful magick user, she hides their movement, and she makes sure that they don't venture near any Earth Guardians territory." Keara quieted and looked a little embarrassed.

"So we are going tomorrow night, why not tonight?" I asked, Tara again looked at me her eyes showed a hidden pain.

"Because Black Mist will be back from the Immortal realm by then, he needs dragon bane for this fight hun." I nodded, dragon bane was a powerful herb that dragons were attracted too, they tended to follow the smell of it, but it was rare and Black Mist must have been using every contact he had made in the Immortal realm to get some.

"So, I say we sleep tonight, as long as possible because you will need it for tomorrow night. You don't mind me crashing here do you?" she asked Keara, whom quickly told her it was alright. Tara took the love seat, explaining that she needed something soft after being in the woods for a month. I understood what it was like too sleep in a dark hard place for a long time so I didn't argue with her. That and she would have won anyway. "Fang, if you would like you can either sleep out here on the floor or . . . I can share, I have a king sized bed, it's plenty big." a small blush ran in too her cheeks as she said it and her heart beat changed a little, I bit my lip from laughing, she was about as shy as I was when talking to a person they might like . . . that is, if she likes me.

"Um, I guess I'll sleep on the bed, my shoulders still a bit stiff and sleeping on the floor probably won't help." Keara agreed to that, and after seeing a good excuse for me sharing a bed with her, the blush trailed away. Even though my shoulder was all the way healed . . . she didn't have to know that right away.

"Well, I am going to head to bed now; I'll see you in a little bit." Keara quickly went in too her room, as though she knew I would want too talk too Tara alone.

"Okay girl, why is Black Mist making the dragons follow him? I could do it." I told her upfront, while we both sat on the love seat.

"He told me too tell you, 'not to argue with him and that he is older and wants to do this for you.' that's it hun, anymore questions?" she asked, her voice traced a bitter line, I could tell she wasn't too happy with Black Mist risking his life either.

"Yea . . . Why couldn't I talk too you for so long?" she turned her head away from me,

"It's a complicated story Cody, I'll tell you someday, but I don't want too right now. Can you understand that?" she turned back too me and a faint glimmer of a tears went around her eyes, I nodded, I didn't want to hear a sad story if Tara was not willing to share it. And I would never force her too.

"Now can I ask you something Cody?" she asked her voice had gone quite, if I hadn't been a werewolf I might not have heard it.

"You know you can ask me anything." I told her my own voice had reached her low volume. "Keara . . . she is a nice girl; I can just tell by looking at her . . . do you have feelings for her?" I was taken back by the question; Tara would never normally ask a question like this so seriously, I tilted my head a little at her.

"Yes, I do . . . its hard for me too admit too her, and I don't want to ask if she likes me back until after this stupid fight." I got it out in the open, I didn't want to tip toe around this issue.

Tara smiled, "Oh Cody, I forgot how bad you are at reading anything magickal . . . I just could never imagine you not feeling it . . . but I can see it." I blinked slowly at her, I had no idea of what she was saying, so I prompted her too go on. "She loves you Cody, as much as you love her, you are bonded, and I haven't seen a true bond like this for a long time." she trailed off; my heart sped up, Keara and I? Life bonded? It was rare, and I had never heard of it happening to Earth Guardians, Tara noticed my heart speeding up.

"You didn't know did you?" her face was puzzled; as though she thought I would have been able too sense it. Is that how Keara read me so well and I seemed to respond so much too her smell?

"Go too her and sleep Cody, you are lucky, don't let anything happen to this or I'll kill ya, you understand that?" her eyes flashed a piercing amber at me. I swallowed hard and put my hands up as though I was pleading with her.

"You know I wouldn't let anything hurt her . . ." I kissed her on the head and gave her another hug.

"Its good too see you again girl." she hugged me back.

"And you boy. Now go too sleep." she shoved me a little off the couch, I smiled at her and went down the little hall way too Keara's bedroom. She wasn't lying she had a king sized bed, her breathing and heart rate told me she was about half asleep when I took off my shirt and changed in too my sweat pants and got in too bed. She stirred a little.

"Fang? You here?" she asked lazily in her sleep, I smiled, and kissed her lightly on the forehead which made her smile.

"Good." she whispered and rolled back over, which told me she had gone too sleep. I lay their looking up at the ceiling, our souls were bonded together forever, and we would never truly love any other person romantically for as long as we lived. And we hadn't even told each other that we liked the other. I almost let out a laugh but stifled it, I didn't want to wake Keara, she was already asleep when my mind finally had quitted for the night.

7

The Plan Begins

DREAMS HADN'T COME too me that night, which was strange, usually my life flooded back to me in a dream like state during the short span that I was normally asleep. Awaking to find Keara curled up by my side brought a groggy smile too my face. Hopefully what Tara had said the night before held true, for that would be the greatest thing in this world to wish for. Glancing at the clock the red numbers burned through the darkness revealing that it was only four in the morning. Rolling out of the bed as quietly as possible, I made my way too the living room where Tara was probably awake as well. Sure enough when getting out there, she was sitting up on the couch shifting through a spell book of Keara's.

"This is interesting magick isn't it?" she asked, I shrugged and sat besides her, she put up the book and smiled, her hair was still tussled from sleep, but over all she looked better with the rest she had gotten. I smiled at her, too see Tara again too have someone tangible from my past that I could be with almost made my mind at ease, even with the impending danger we were getting in too. But there was still one thing nagging at my mind.

"Tara, I need to know something, how hard would it be too keep Keara out of the fight." I winced at how I said it, Tara might take it as cowardice and scold me for it, I was the whipping boy again, and she the master of these plans. Taking in a large even breath Tara looked at me with her knowing eyes that kept contact with my own.

"We need her Cody, no way we can do this without another good magick user, I can only do so much hun." my mind raced, to have Keara in the midst of this battle made my stomach tighten, she was human in all aspects, well except with her knowledge of magicks. I was almost unstoppable in a fight, as long as the person I was fighting didn't have silver, I would take down almost any enemy, get almost any wound and still bounce back from it. Tara tried to smile, tried to give me that-everything-will-be-okay look, I hated when she did that but I could never tell her.

"I know how much it sucks too see her in a fight, but she is an Earth Guardian Cody, and we need her for this." I sighed and sunk back in too the couch which had acquired Tara's spicy smell, cinnamon, that was the best way I could describe it.

"So, how is this plan gonna work again?" she looked relieved with the change of subject, she ran it by me again.

"Oh and hun, I brought this for Keara I figured she wouldn't have one." Reaching behind the pillow on the couch Tara brought out a small hand gun, I took in a sharp intake of air, almost sounding like a hiss. Keara had told me once how she feared guns, and just by my reaction Tara knew Keara wouldn't like this.

"It's a good safety measure, yes Keara has good magicks, but silver is the best thing for taking down any Were creature. She might need this incase she cant use a spell or something." she handed it too me, I sighed and took it, I had no idea of how Tara brought it in with her wearing as little as she had, but I never questioned that about her, she was resourceful. Not knowing anything about guns I didn't ask Tara how too use it, I knew she would explain it too Keara when needed. As though Keara knew she was being talked about she shuffled out of the room, one hand rubbing the sleep out of her eyes.

"I can't believe you two are awake at this time. You Were creatures are so silly." she mumbled as she made her way too the coffee maker and turned it on. Tara voted to have a cup as well, I had never seen Tara on anything with caffeine but I figured it would be entertaining. Standing up slowly, I brought the gun over too Keara, her eyes grew wide as she backed up.

"Where the hell did you get that Fang!" her voice was strained, I looked too Tara to explain, and without asking she told Keara her idea for the gun.

"But what if I hit Fang with it? Or you or Black Mist . . . no, this wont end well." I set the gun down on the counter, it seemed to bother her a lot, and her eyes were wild when she stared at it. As though the thing would be alive and try to bite her, but even I knew that it took another creature too wield it.

"Keara, listen, if you don't want too use it, you don't have too, Tara just thinks it will be smarter . . . I wont force you." Tara slipped in too my mind

"Don't say that, she will need it!"

I sent a growl to her and she quickly backed off, Keara took a long shaky breath in and let it out slowly, I kept my distance from her. When a person has a fear of something, sometimes it will rub off or they can interpret things differently.

"I'll use it . . . we might need It." her voice was shaking, so were her hands, I moved forward too her, to give her comfort of some sort. She allowed it as I put my arms around her small frame.

JOURNEY THROUGH THE DARK WOODS | 95

"Its okay luv, nothing bad will happen, its just a safety net incase the shit hit's the fan." she let out a dry laugh against my chest. I rested my chin on the top of her head; she was short enough for me to do that. Tara got up from the couch.

"Well, if you guys would wait for a little bit, I will be right back, you have sheltered me for the night Keara, so breakfast is on me." with that she left without waiting for a reply from either of us.

Keara was the first too pull away, her eyes were rimmed with tears.

"I'm sorry I acted like that, but those things bring the worst out in me, ever sense Gran first told me about my parents . . ." she trailed off and shook her head as she poured water in too a kettle and set it on a burner. I didn't reply, I waited for her too say more, Tara had had break downs on me before, I knew too be quite until either she asked me something or the topic changed. She continued to babble.

"But I guess it is a good idea too use it, I mean, like Tara practically pointed out, I am not as experienced as her in a fight with magick, and I am only human after all. I can't do the things you do." she was continuing to go around the kitchen pulling out mugs and a thing of tea bags. She remembered that I didn't like coffee that brought a grin too my face and I decided to talk to her and change the topic for her.

"I don't think you'll need to use it, Tara is confident that nothing bad should happen. In and out, that's all. And after wards, I say we go to a pub and get smashed." most people whom had any knowledge of Were creatures knew it took a lot for them to get smashed. But I was hoping the joke would break Keara of her fears of the firearm.

"I am actually going to agree with that one . . . can I ask you a question?" I again reassured her that she never needed to ask that and I would answer anything she wanted too know to the best of my knowledge.

"The full moon . . . its pretty close, will that help this battle, will it increase your strength? None of my books can tell me that." I tilted my head a little at her, as the kettle let out a gush of steam; Keara pulled it off the burner and went about fixing tea. The coffee wasn't done yet.

"Well, in a way, I guess it will. It doesn't increase my strength; it makes me less of a human than I already am, that's about it." I was trying to be blunt about it, the full moon was a terrible thing for me, and I never really remembered what I did on those nights, just bits and pieces like a nightmare.

"What do you mean . . . less human?" she asked, her eyes looked up, searching my face for the answer; I breathed in heavily . . . fear? I smelled fear on her, was she afraid of me? On what I might say . . . she knew I wasn't human, how could this scare her more. The beast inside of me sent a shudder through my body, fear and blood, those were great things to make any Were creatures beast come too life. Keara noticed the shudder; her eyes grew a bit wider.

"Fang what's wrong?" I took a step away from her that smell of fear still wafted from her, like a blanket that would drown me, and allow my beast to spring free. I took a couple of steps back and closed my eyes; counting slowly to ten I opened them again. "You smell like fear Keara . . . you know that I am not human, and around these times there are only two things that will make me want to hurt you . . . that is fear and blood . . . this will be hard for you, but you cant be afraid of me when its close too the full moon." I whispered these words, but my voice was huskier then it normally was, the beast waited, it wanted too tear free of me, and attack the thing that smelled so sweetly of fear. Keara nodded slowly, her shields went up like a magickal slap too the face, I took a long shuddering breath and sat down on one of the chairs at her small kitchen table. I buried my face in too my hands, not wanting too look at her fearful eyes.

"I'm sorry." I whispered, a mug was set in front of me, and another chair squeaked as it slide across the floor, looking up, Keara was sitting by me, her mug of coffee in one hand. Mine smelled sharply of peppermint, I breathed it in, trying to get the last of Keara's fear out of my nose.

"I keep forgetting that your not human . . . I know it's silly. I didn't know that this close to the full moon it was hard for you too control yourself around some things. I am sorry about that, I shouldn't of over reacted." it was only three days till the full moon but already that impending thing nagged at my spirit and beast.

"Its okay, I should have told you, its hard for me sometimes, Tara is lucky, her beast isn't as blood thirsty as mine . . ." I took the mug and sipped at the hot liquid as it burned down my throat, I sighed in too it and Keara took another sip from hers.

"I'm not afraid of you Fang, I am afraid of what could happen to you on the full moon, that's why I asked . . . and I shouldn't have been afraid. I know you wont hurt me." she touched my shoulder lightly, another shudder ran through me, this one was not for the need to hunt and feed, but just for being physically close to another person. Were creatures gained a lot from physical touch, it could even be used to help heal us. Keara seemed intent to finish her coffee before starting another conversation, even though her shields were up, I knew something was bothering her. I just couldn't put my finger on it, I might be over a thousand years old . . . but even I can't read women.

"Why did you wake up so early anyway?" I finally asked, trying to steer the starting conversation to something less thought provoking. She set down the mug, and gave me her full attention.

"Well, you're like a built in heater, and when you got up, I woke up because there wasn't anymore warmth. I got cold, so I figured I might as well get up." I hid the grin behind my mug as I finished the last of the tea, I had gotten that a lot actually, when I was a roguish type wolf, I had been with some interesting people and all of them had said that I either gave off too much heat or just the right amount. Tara once called me a mobile blanket. A light chuckle escaped my lips, Keara looked more confused, but I decided not too tell her that other women had told me the same thing, not a good way to start the morning. Before I could continue Tara came through the door with a large grocery bag.

"Who's hungry?"

JOURNEY THROUGH THE DARK WOODS

Breakfast was eggs with bell peppers mixed in, bacon, sausage and croissants, it was a very large and filling meal, Tara and I ate most of it while Keara just took one plate and was satisfied.

"When is Black Mist going to get back?" I asked, and while I asked it I felt another metaphysical door open in my mind and Black Mist's voice whispered

"I'll be in soon, Tara gave me the address, save me some food." and the door shut, I smiled, Tara had the same sleepy smile on her face as well. Keara looked confused.

"I take it Black Mist talked to you both?" she asked, I felt bad for her, it was so easy for me too talk to them, but Keara couldn't be part of this. Her magick was a different flavor then Tara's.

"Yea, he did, he'll be in soon." I said, as I finished a glass of milk. It's hard to fill up a werewolf but Tara had once cooked for both Black Mist and I, so she knew how to make large portions. After breakfast, Keara asked if we wanted showers before we left, Tara laughed at this.

"Oh girl, you don't know much about being in the forest do ya?" she stated bluntly, Tara had never really understood the need for tact around some people. She had been referring to the soapy smell that would easily be recognized by the other werewolves more easily then our normal scents. Keara blushed a little and turned to cleaning up the kitchen so we couldn't see that she was embarrassed. I opened the mental door to Tara,

"Don't do that too her, you know she doesn't understand a lot about this stuff." I scowled her, she gave me a small pout she didn't know that she had said anything wrong. I let it go.

"Hey Keara . . ." before I finished my sentence, Black Mist came through the door, his black hair was still tied back but strands had fallen out. His face was slightly ashen, and his golden eyes dark.

"Did you save me any food?" he asked, as he stumbled in too the kitchen, Tara moved faster then me and grabbed his arm so he wouldn't fall over. Keara on cue brought over a heaping plate of food for him that we had saved.

"What happened Darrick?" Tara asked him, while she sat by him, Darrick was his human name; Tara was weird and never used our werewolf names. Black Mist stopped for a second from his food to speak.

"I teleported myself too the Immortal realm for the dragon bane . . . I got it but I had too teleport out faster then I thought. It seems the bounty on my head in that realm hasn't gone away yet." he let out a dry choked chuckle, as he continued too eat.

"So, you used up your energy, you idiot, you could die doing that." Tara sneered at him, Black Mist didn't seem to listen too her.

"We could wait a day for you too rest and then do this?" Keara asked, slightly unsure from the corner of the kitchen.

"NO, we have to go tonight! I've been putting this off too long . . . all I have to do is distract some fucking dragons . . ." he coughed as he chocked down his food.

Tara looked up at me, her eyes full of worry, and her love for Black Mist shown through her face.

"At least we don't have too go until tonight, you can sleep until then." I pointed out, trying to help Tara with her worry; Black Mist finished the plate of food, and stood up.

"Yes, that would be good." he put his dish in too the sink, his hand was shaking slightly as he did it.

"You can have the bedroom, just let me grab out some stuff." Keara offered and walked out of the kitchen before Black Mist could say anything. He smiled and opened the door to our minds.

"She is very sweet Cody, take care of her." his eyes were full of some odd emotion, I could never read Black Mist, and I had no idea what emotion he was conveying, so I simply nodded my head. Keara came back out with an armful of clothes and set them on the couch, she also had my knapsack. Black Mist gave her his thanks and exited too the bedroom, Tara was behind him. Keara gave her an odd look but I knew that Tara's warmth would help him recover. I told Keara of this and she nodded.

"So if I got injured you're warmth could help me heal?" she looked puzzled, I chuckled and started to wash the dishes she followed and was drying them off for me.

"No, you aren't a Were creature of any sort, with Were creatures another persons warmth can help their bodies heal wounds or sickness. It's because when we are injured our body temperature goes up, more than normal, for the healing process. So another person's warmth added to that helps." I felt like an encyclopedia for Were creatures, I seemed to be explaining a lot too Keara these days. I wondered why none of her books talked about these things. Keara nodded and seemed to digest the information given too her.

"Oh, okay when you are injured my body temperature could help heal it? Sort of like with your shoulder, that's why you laid down besides me, Right?" she asked, a blush crept over my face, had she woken up and found me by her? Before she could say anymore I nodded and continued scrubbing the dishes. After the dishes were done, Tara came out of the bedroom, she looked confused.

"He is so stubborn." she whispered. "I'm gonna be staying in there with him too make sure he sleeps, we'll be out before dusk." she told us then retreated back in too the bedroom. Keara also looked worried.

"What if he can't do it?" Keara asked, her voice hushed, I shook my head.

"He will."

8

Into the Fray

AFTER A VERY uneventful day, it was finally drawing towards dusk, Black Mist and Tara emerged from the bedroom. Black Mist looked better but he wasn't a hundred percent yet. Keara seemed about as concerned as I was; she paced and cleaned the apartment while they had been asleep.

"We need too head out, we can teleport to the edge of Kofra's territory . . . but from there we must walk. I will separate from you three and head to the dragons. But I will be in touch, Tara can you set up the spell?" Black Mist's voice was hallow as though the magick he had used earlier had taken more out of him then he had told us.

"Yea I was planning on it hun." Tara mumbled and sat down in the center of the living room.

"I need all three of you over here, as long as your all touching me this should work." she said, I went over and sat down beside her, Keara came second and grabbed my hand lightly, Black Mist sat on the other side of Tara and took her hand. Closing her eyes, the magick started spilling around us, I felt the pull and twist of it gliding across my skin, I closed my eyes, and allowed it too play out. I had been teleported before, so I knew that the weird pulling feeling would come, then the feeling of movement. My stomach jerked and I could feel a cold breeze on my face.

"We're here." Black Mist whispered, I opened my eyes too see Black Mist kissing Tara gently on the cheek and heading off in to the surrounding forest. I looked away too see that Keara was slowly standing up. Tara got up too,

"Follow me." she whispered, as she ducked down in too the darkness,

99

"Let's go." Holding out my hand to Keara, I knew she couldn't see well in the darkness so I lead her through it. I felt my eyes bleed to a wolf's, it reflected the light better then my normal eyes, and made sure that I didn't lead Keara in too a tree.

"Its so dark." she whispered, I chuckled lightly, and looked behind me, I could clearly see Keara's face, and I smiled even though I knew she couldn't see it.

"You know it's sort of freaky when you do that." she whispered, I looked back, and followed Tara's scent ahead of me.

"What my eyes?" I asked, I looked back again at her and she nodded.

"Well its better then us running in to a tree." I told her, she laughed a little at that. I figured that my eyes glowing back at her in the dark must be an interesting sight indeed, so I didn't push it. Shoving through the foliage we found ourselves in a small clearing, Tara was crouched down in the darkness.

"Good, you're here, okay, Cody, there is one guard up ahead, I'd love for you too put on you're war paint and go get 'em." she said, Keara looked confused, and I simply patted her on the head like an innocent child.

"What? I don't get it?" she whispered back, Tara laughed lightly,

"He's gonna go make sure the guard doesn't stop us." she responded, looking back at Keara, I smiled

"I'm going up ahead, stay with Tara . . ." I went off in too the darkness before she could respond. In the darkness where I knew Keara couldn't see me, I focused my mind on the simple spell for keeping my clothes with me while I changed shape. The beast was happy and exploded out of my body in a rush of heat and fur. I knew that in my half form, I resembled a large half man half wolf, I had hands, curved in claws, and I could even speak. Slinking through the forest, I smelled the guard up ahead, he was young, and in his half form as well, I was down wind of him, he couldn't even hear me. I felt the door in my mind open and Tara's voice whispered through me

"Stay in that form until I tell ya, I don't know if there will be more guards anywhere." I sent a laugh too her, she closed the door. I crept forward, my paws digging in too the soft under growth. As soon as I was close enough and could almost hear him breathing in my ear, I sprung. Before he could even let out a growl, my teeth met his throat, and I pulled. Blood spilled out over his body and some on to me. His eyes turned up in too his skull, as he fell to the ground. Spitting out the ruined flesh, I tore in too his chest, right under the rib cage. A werewolf can still come back from a throat being ripped out, but we can't live without our hearts. I pushed my claws through his ribs and found the frantically beating organ. I squeezed it between my fingers and pulled it out with a sickening sucking noise.

"Okay Tara, he's dead." I whispered to her, she didn't reply, she didn't need too. I carefully picked up the body and pushed it too the foliage of the fringe of the clearing. I didn't want Keara to trip over a dead body . . . especially a body that I had made. I could hear Keara coming through the thick forest, while I whipped most of

JOURNEY THROUGH THE DARK WOODS

the blood off of me with the leaves around me. Soon Keara was in the clearing with me, she couldn't see me that well, I still crouched in the tree line.

"Fang?" she asked, I stepped out of the trees, she turned too me.

"Oh so that's what she meant." she smiled, "Well I guess it makes sense for you too stay like that incase of more guards." she stepped closer too me, out of instinct I took a step back.

"What's wrong?" she asked, her head tilting in a confused gesture. I looked down. "You're one of the few women who didn't run screaming from me . . . its weird for you too be close to me while I am like this." my voice was a low rusty growl, it didn't sound anything like my normal voice or even a human's. Keara laughed, I didn't understand, my ears pricked forward.

"You're afraid I am going to run from you? Oh Fang, I saw you kill Talon back in the Darkwoods, nothing you could do would scare me away from you."

I nodded slowly, she had seen my true demon, she had seen it and not run screaming, not like the other girls, the very thought brought warmth too my heart.

"I'm sorry, sometimes I don't know how to act around you." she stepped closer too me, this time I didn't move back, it was hard, but I stood my ground.

"Just act like yourself." she whispered, as she held up her hand too me, I stood as still as death, my heart raced, luckily she couldn't hear it. She leaned her hand forward and put it on my cheek.

"You sort of feel like a big dog." she said, as she searched my face, I managed a laugh, but in this shape it sounded like a choked growl, she pulled back at that.

"I'm sorry; I can't laugh very well in this form." I told her, she laughed for me, I smiled back at her, but as I had just explained, this form wasn't good for human gestures; it was more of a bearing of teeth.

"So what are we waiting for?" I asked, Keara turned from me and looked back at the other clearing where Tara was.

"She is channeling the spell to make the wards of Kofra's fortress go down, and for Black Mist's sign." just at that moment a piercing screech shifted through the forest, Keara jumped, she stepped back suddenly, and almost feel over. I reached out too her, and grabbed her around the waist. She didn't run from me, she didn't cower, she just looked grateful that I caught her. She sighed.

"That was a red dragon." I whispered to her, she pushed off of me to stand up.

"Thank you and I have never heard a dragon before. How big are they?" she asked, staring in too the darkness, I scented the air, a dragon smelled of sulfur, I breathed in heavily, there were two of them, one female one male, a mated pair, they were young too.

"They are about the size of very large horses. Red dragons have small wings only for gliding and balance it makes them easier too control." I told her, Keara nodded; I felt magick tingle through the air.

"Tara must be setting up the spell." Keara whispered her voice was breathy. Was she afraid? I couldn't tell she had shielded that for my own benefits. I heard Tara through my mind

"Change back, there are no guards coming." I smiled again, and told Keara what she had said, I changed back, luckily the simple spell was still in place and I was fully dressed. Keara questioned this, I told her of how Tara had taught it too Black Mist and I, and she blushed lightly and agreed it was a smart idea. Energy escaped from my muscles, changing too often could drain your energy faster then spell casting.

"Are you okay?" she asked, putting a hand on my shoulder.

"Yea, just changed too fast, I'll be fine." Keara patted me lightly on the shoulder. The metaphysical door opened again.

"You guys need to head out now; I got the wards lowered, but only for like half an hour!" I relayed the message to Keara, she swallowed, and turned too me.

"I guess we have to end this tonight." and with that we headed through the darkness.

9

The Changing of a Soul

KEARA TRAILED BEHIND me, her hand in mine, it was sweating but I didn't blame her, this was going to be a good fight or a quick one . . . or everything would explode and the shit would hit the fan. I bared my teeth at the darkness almost mocking it; I knew its master was ahead of me, in that quite fortress. In that old mansion that held so many memories, it was large with two top floors and a very large basement, not many went down their. Only Kofra's victims and new werewolves were allowed down there. I scented the air, at this time of month, near the full moon, a lot of the werewolves took off for a week, leaving the fortress with only a handful of guards and the Alphas. Tasting the smells in the air, I knew the guards were rushing after the dragons; I said a little prayer for Black Mist's safety and pressed on. I wasn't a very religious guy, but I knew there was something bigger then me pulling the strings of fate and I wanted them to protect my old friend. Keara feel behind me, dropping my hand, I whirled on my heels and bent low to the ground.

"Are you okay?" I asked her, my eyes still that of a wolf's, so I could see her in the darkness,

"Yea you started to go faster, my foot caught on a root, but I'm alright." helping her too her feet I set out again and controlled my pace for her. She was magickal and immortal yes, but she was also human, she didn't have my senses. The trees started to become sparse as we headed towards the strong hold, my senses strained around the area, the mansion loomed ahead of us, large and foreboding. It had been built long ago, at least two hundred years after I joined, made of stones and mortar.

103

Looking like a medieval strong hold, it was strong enough too withstand a young werewolf's first change, and more magickally endowed than any building I had ever known. But I knew what sort of things had happened in that place, rape, torture, mutilation, all for the Daligulven's reign over this territory. My stomach complained as we continued to get closer, too many bad memories. We stood behind the last tree next to the mansion, sniffing the air; I knew all the guards had followed the dragons I just needed to find Kofra's scent. A nauseous mixture of thyme and lilies, it was an odd aroma, but it was unique so it was easier to pick out. The faint smell tickled my nose, I suppressed a sneeze. Keara's hand gripped mine harder, though she was hiding her fear from me I knew it gripped her stomach as it did mine. "Let's go." I whispered, she didn't reply, we headed through the still open double doors, their was a large room before us, it was where we had had meals and 'entertainment' in the old days, but now it looked more like a perverted shrine. And the smell of blood swallowed all of my senses, I stumbled back at it, it was too thick in the air. What had Kofra been doing? Keara put a hand on my other arm.

"Fang? What's wrong!?" Her voice was frantic and was very quite, she knew I could hear her.

"It's the smell luv . . . its blood, like a thousand people were slaughtered here." my voice was hoarse, as though I had been choking. She gripped my arm, as I gripped her hand back,

"Come on." I shifted through the smell of blood, as I stared at the large throne that looked like a pagan alter in the center of the room. Had Kofra fallen to the darkness that gripped us all? Or had she thought herself a goddess and wanted sacrifices? I had no answers to these questions that kept slipping through my mind. "Concentrate." I breathed heavily and fought to find her scent. It was leading upstairs, in to the rooms, it was where everyone was housed, though most shared a bedroom, like a dorm almost, I on the other hand had had my own. No one wanted to bunk with the miserable Aukoc. I pulled Keara along the stairs, my heart racing, so was hers, it echoed mine, upon reaching the top of the stairs, my heart skipped some beats, as a flash of light blinded us both, falling to the ground, I felt magick grip my mind . . .

Spots raced over my vision, as I tried to move my arms, they were tied up above me, and upon pulling I felt the sharp burn of the silver chains cutting in to my wrists. I let out a grunt of pain, as I did that a laugh traced the air. It was light and airy, just as the voice would be, with a thick accent of a woman whom was originally French.

"Kofra" I spat the words, she stood in front of me, her blonde hair done in a modern long hair cut, flowing past her shoulders. Her enticing dark green eyes trailed over my face, she was tall and thin, but all that body was covered in well developed muscle. All the men of the pack had fallen to her at one point, sadly I had also been one of them, and she had broken my mind and body more then once.

JOURNEY THROUGH THE DARK WOODS

"Oh Silver Fang, how I have missed you." she whispered, as her fingers traced over my face, I snapped at her, baring my teeth.

"Shhhh, bad doggie, biting your master Tsk tsk, and you even brought me such a nice gift, that sweet little Earth Guardian, all alone in that room . . . Mmmm what I could do with her." she purred in to my ear, my heart sank, and it must have shown on my face for Kofra's intoxicating laugh filled my mind.

"No, not her." I whispered, she smiled, and it was not anything to make her face more beautiful but to make you terrified as to what was behind those dark eyes.

"Do you remember why I allowed you to stay in the pack Hmm?" her hand played lightly through my hair, as her fingers trailed down my now exposed chest . . . she had removed my shirt, but luckily had left my pants. Their was another cold chain around my waist and my feet, she knew how to restrain a wolf, if I tried too change, it would of killed me. My mind raced for the answer to her question.

I snarled, "Yea, it was my eyes, an opposite of yours, light green to your dark, you liked how I looked Kofra . . . but you knew you couldn't have me." Kofra had always been a proud bitch and to hurt her pride was to make her angry, and when she was angry she might slip. The smile curved in to a fierce bearing of teeth, her canines were pointed like a vampire, she had spent too much time in her wolf form at one point and now she was not completely human looking, her finger nails were even curved a little in to claws, she was a frightening creature.

"Yes Silver Fang, that is the reason, those pretty eyes of yours." her hand trailed lower across my body, I tried to push away from her, she giggled, though the sound only held malice.

"You don't want my touch? How sad, you once loved it little one." she put both of her hands on either side of my face, pulling me towards her.

"Now listen Silver Fang, I give you one option, come back to me, and be my Alpha, rule this territory with me. We could be so powerful." her face softened in to a mask of innocence, though power burned through her eyes.

"NO!" I spat in her face, she licked her lips and smiled again.

"Fine then, you will do something for me even if you don't want too. You will be mine again. Even if you don't want it, I found a way to take something away from you." she pushed forward and kissed me, her fangs nicking my lips, the irony taste of blood pooled over my tongue as she continued the kiss. I fought back, but she was strong and I was restrained. Magick welled up around us, I felt something low in my chest pull, it hurt, the pain made me scream, but Kofra's mouth covered mine. Tears streamed down my face, as the pain coursed through my being, the silver cut further in to my wrists as I tried to break free. The pain was too much . . . and then there was darkness . . .

I awoke again, but this time, there was no pain and no guilt, anger and hatred filled my heart, the need to hunt and to kill made my eyes bleed to a wolf's. I growled low in my chest, as I moved my aching arms in front of me. I was unchained, and

Kofra stood in front of me. But instead of being afraid of her, she was as lovely as she was when I had first met her.

"Did you return to me Silver Fang?" she purred, I nodded, and a smile crossed my lips, I was free, free of that miserable soul making me so weak with guilt. I stood up, and trailed a hand across Kofra's face; she smiled and nuzzled my palm.

"What would you have me do Mistress?" my voice was lower but still thick with an accent, she smiled and it even reached her eyes.

"There is a girl in this place, she misses you and is so afraid without you. Maybe you should teach her to be afraid . . . hmmm?" she told me, I laughed, full of bitterness and disgust, that human, Keara, oh she was going to be fun.

Kofra had led me to the room where Keara was held, I opened it as Kofra left again, while she said she would return shortly, to see the aftermath. Keara was sitting in the corner, her head on her knees. She looked up, the hair fell away from her face, something made me hesitate, but I pushed through it, and walked in to the room.

"Fang! Oh thank God she didn't get you, I just thought it was Me." she started to walk towards me but stopped, did she already sense that I was different?

"Oh no, it was both of us, but she sent me up here to . . . check on you." my voice was a low growl, Keara stepped back.

"Fang what's wrong?" she asked, her voice started to quiver, her shields were strong so the over powering feel of her fear didn't fall from her, but her scent told me it was starting to break.

"Mmmm you smell so good Keara, almost good enough for a snack, or a play thing." I continued to walk towards her, she kept back tracking, but my legs were longer then hers, I was soon standing in front of her. Her back was pressed up against the wall, her eyes were wide, and the smell of fear perfumed the air around us.

"Don't, Fang this isn't you." she pleaded, I felt the laugh creep up out of my mouth and rattle out from my teeth, her eyes grew larger, so much white in those creamy chocolate eyes.

"Oh this is me, this is the one who helped you're dear little Fang survive all those years, no one can survive if they have guilt and fear." I traced a finger along her cheek; she flinched as though it burned, the beast in side of me was eager to be released, so it could see if this treat was as appetizing as it smelled. Sweat feel down her face, as the fear started too slip through her barriers. Sniffing softly, I leaned forward, I wanted it, that fear that flavor, she started too move away from me. Grabbing hold of her chin with my hand I forced her too stay, kissing her forehead I licked my lips; the taste of fear sent a shiver through me. She spoke softly, her voice so meager and tantalizing, it made me look at her again.

"No, you taught me people could change, and you were . . . so brave and caring, you're not the Fang I know, but I know he is still in there." I paused, my hand still on her chin, I stroked my thumb over her lips, they were dry she gasped and turned

JOURNEY THROUGH THE DARK WOODS | 107

her head away. "FANG COME BACK TO ME!" she yelled, I tilted my head, why was I doing this? I shook the thought from my mind, she turned back to me.

"You're in there . . . I know it." she said, her voice regaining some of its calm, she pushed an arm against me, startling me, I stepped back, she pulled the loaded pistol out of her belt loops.

"Get away from me." she stared down at me from the gun, her hands trembling lightly. Another laugh bubbled from my mouth.

"You wont shoot me, not after all of the things we've been through, fuck I even think you care about me . . . I know I did, but that's gone now." she stepped forward the gun pointed at my chest, her eyes looking towards me.

"I love you Fang." she whispered, I stopped, my whole body froze, those simple words, why did they make my heart feel different. Something pushed at my mind, I love her too it whispered, I shoved it aside and let a rage filled scream echo out of me.

"I don't love her!" I screamed, I pushed at myself and lunged, Boom! Pain coursed through my arm, the bullet had grazed me. I stopped, falling to the floor, panting, I love her, I can't hurt her, she is the one, the voice kept yelling kept pushing, I could hear Keara. "Fang, oh God Fang I'm Sorry, I had too, please come back to Me." hands were on me, someone holding me caressing my hair, holding the wound on my arm. Warmth flooded through me and then pain, I gripped hold of the only warm thing by me, her scent washed over me, basil and lavender, the greatest smell in the world, and I kept hearing her speak.

"I love you, don't leave me." I closed my eyes; tears had started to well from them. Guilt, pain, remorse, everything washed over me. But I still had her, holding me, loving me for who I was.

"Keara, oh God, I love you." I whispered, my throat burned, and the tears still flowed from my eyes, twice I had broken in front of her, and twice she had held me.

"Are you back?" she asked, looking down at me, I was practically lying in her lap, her eyes full of tears as well.

"Yes . . ." I whispered, she hugged me tighter and I returned it, it had happened, she had said she loved me, and I her, it wasn't as bad as I thought.

My mind raced with what had happened, I couldn't imagine myself doing anything like that to Keara, yet she had stayed by me, and fought against the evil the once ruled me. She straightened up, a puzzled look spread across her face,

"What if Kofra comes back in here?" she asked, her voice still breathy and shaky, I slowly stood up and brought her with me, Kofra had indeed told me she would come back in too see the 'aftermath' I sniffed the air, her scent was still cold on the outside of the door.

"We have a little time, we have to act this out well luv or she will kill us both or seriously hurt one of us. You need to act as frightened as you can, pretend like I am going to hurt you, and I will assist in the affect." I concentrated and brought my beast a little to the surface, I felt a slight change, as my nails became claws, and my eyes bleed yellow. I could feel my hair growing out a bit more and other random changes taking place through my body. It was a short shift, something to use in a fight for intimidation, only older werewolves could make this sort of change, and it took years of practice. Keara's eyes grew wide again; I smiled, baring teeth that were now fangs.

"Good, you need to be afraid of me; I am after all a beast." I growled, my voice had also changed, going down an octave. I sniffed the air again, I could smell Kofra faintly down stairs, and she was on the move.

"Be afraid of me Keara, show me fear." I shouted at her, she stumbled back a little bit, but caught herself on the wall again. "When I give you a wink shoot Kofra with that pistol, aim for the heart or head. Hide it behind your back again." I pointed to the gun on the ground, she quickly picked it up, Kofra's scent became heavier.

"Don't take any of this seriously luv, this is too save our skins." I smiled at her the best I could with fangs, she nodded back, still shaking, I heard the door knob turn.

"You stupid girl, you thought I loved you?" I snarled and growled at her, I heard Kofra's dulcet laugh behind me, I turned a little to look at her, her arms were crossed in front of her, it had made her cleavage stand out even more in the tight shirt she wore.

"Oh Silver Fang, good you haven't killed her, I wanted to watch." she purred, I licked my lips and crept behind her, Keara was still up against the wall.

"You bitch you did this!" her voice was shaky yet had a little power behind it, thank God she was already scared to begin with or this would have been hard.

"I was waiting for you pet." I whispered, trailing my hand over her shoulder, rolling her head a little to the side she smiled at me.

"Good, I am quite sorry little witch, but I have more need of him then you do, he would make a lovely alpha." she stroked a hand across my arm; I shuddered under her warm touch.

"No, he can't be gone." Keara protested, I smirked, by this time I was already behind Kofra, my hands resting lightly on her shoulders, I pulled her against me, she stumbled, she was actually surprised, and I smiled.

"Don't struggle pet." I winked at Keara, I heard the blast and felt the impact of Kofra's body against mine, her head rolled to me a clean bullet wound was on her forehead.

"You . . . you have it back . . . but how?" she whispered, then her eyes shut, and she became limp, dropping her to the ground I proceeded to shut the beast away and look human again. Keara stood there, shaking, her arms out stretched with the gun in her trembling hands.

"Keara? Are you alright?" I whispered, she blinked and dropped the gun. I watched it fall, while my vision blurred I felt a metaphysical door blow open, as pain poured through my body, my body retched and I threw my head back in pain. Keara ran towards me, but my eyes had blurred with the pain, it left me panting on

JOURNEY THROUGH THE DARK WOODS

the ground, clutching at something large and invisible above me, holding me down, crushing me . . . I could hear Tara screaming and Keara's voice ringing through my head. The pain snapped the door shut up, and something broke, the invisible pressure vanished, I was left lying on the ground panting,

"Oh Lord, Fang are you okay?" Keara asked me, and again she was holding me, and all that could escape my trembling lips was.

"Black Mist . . . he's dead."

10

Her Suffering

TARA HAD BLOWN the door wide open, she was screaming, her pain rattled my body, as Keara was trying to shake some sense in too me.

"What do you mean, he can't be dead?!" she kept asking, using as much concentration as possible, I yelled back at Tara.

"Where are you!?" she didn't reply, she kept screaming and crying, her heart was burning, shaking my own head to clear the yelling, I shoved the door closed. Silence rung through my head, I could hear the blood pulsing through my ears; Keara had tears running down her face.

"He's not dead is he?" she asked, I looked up at her; the look alone told her it was true, a sob escaped her lips. Why was she so broken up about this, she didn't know Black Mist as well as I did, pushing those thoughts away. I stood upon shaky legs and headed towards the door, the first light of dawn was peeking through the world. Keara followed, we both ran out of the mansion, I was first out, Keara was slower then I, sniffing the air, I caught hold of Tara's scent, that sweet cinnamon smell was so close. Keara stood gasping beside me; she had run as fast as she could.

"She's this way." I told her, and headed off, we made our way through the trees again, and found another overly large clearing, the tingle of magick danced upon my skin, Keara shuddered besides me. Tara was in the middle, her back to me, and Black Mist's body in her arms. She was still screaming, her soul mate had died, and her heart wanted to follow. I ran up too her, and almost feel back with what had happened. Black Mist was torn open, like a rag doll, his face was bloody, and his entrails had been ripped out of him, the smell alone almost made me gag. A dragon holds a lot of magick, and their maw and claws can not be healed by a werewolf.

"Tara?" I whispered, leaning down beside her, she didn't look at me, she kept staring at him, her eyes were hallowed and her face was as pale as death itself.

"Tara, I know, he's gone, but we're alive, we have too make it . . . we love you Tara, come back to me." I whispered in to her ear, and kissed her hair lightly. Tara was my sister, she was my friend, and at one point she had even been my lover, but right now she was my family, and I had to help her. Her sobs continued but she had stopped screaming, I sighed, and put an arm around her shoulders and buried my face in her neck.

"I love you Tara, don't leave me alone." I told her, her sobs succeeded, she turned to me, I pulled my face away, and she blinked.

"Cody . . . Darrick is gone." she whispered, I nodded, and pulled her away from his ruined body.

"We'll bury him luv." I told her, I didn't know what to say to her like this, she was so frail.

"No, I'll do it." she stood, her legs trembling beneath her, taking my arm, she put her hand out before her, pointing at Black Mist. A swirl of magick erupted from the ground, as it took him under.

"He's protected now." she whispered, as she nearly collapsed. Taking her in too my arms, she was so small, so frail, she had used too much magick and had felt a blow worse then death.

"Will she be alright?" I heard Keara behind me; I turned with Tara still in my arms.

"Yea she needs rest, and as much love as we can give her." I told her.

"At least I got a hot bath and a warm bed at home that might help her." Keara whispered, as she came to stand besides me. Kofra was dead but at what price, my greatest friend's heart was a mess, and her love was dead. Keara knew I loved her, but she had seen me as the evil bastard I once was. Even in Death, Kofra still made life hard for Tara and me.

Keara had insisted that we search the mansion for the tools that Kofra was going too use against the humans so that the Daligulven tribe could never use them. She had left me alone too watch over Tara as she slept in my arms. Finally after a half hour, Keara came out and shook her head.

"There was nothing there . . . I even used spells to find any items containing magick . . . but nothing . . . maybe she hid them." attempting too shrug with Tara's frame in my arms, we both agreed to just return to the flat.

Upon returning, we got Tara in too a bed, and left her too sleep, we were going to join her there in a second. Keara brewed some tea, and set it before me. Chamomile with mint, to calm and relax, she knew what I needed. She poured herself a mug and sat besides me.

"That was one wild ride . . . I wonder if all Earth Guardians have to face things like this." she whispered in to her cup. I tried to smile but I still had the smell of Black Mist's blood in my nose.

"No, other Earth Guardians are loners and only seek help within the council; you have friends outside of the council." I patted her shoulder lightly; she took my hand while setting her mug down with the other.

"I have more then that, what I said back there was true. You're the only person I have ever trusted fully . . ." she trailed off, but kept a hold of me, this time I did smile.

"Same . . . I've never met anyone like you. Not sense I was human." I ended it there, she knew what had happened to the first girl I had truly loved and how the rouge wolf had killed her, and then turned me.

"Tara told me, that we have what her and . . ." I couldn't say his name but Keara nodded and had me continue. "What they had, that we're soul mates, she could just tell by looking at us." I whispered the last bit; I was embarrassed I had never just come out and said that I liked a girl before. Keara looked down, she was chewing on her lip, thinking.

"It sounds right, I felt so much, when he died, and I thought that the magick had spread to me. Maybe we are?" she made it a question, I shrugged, I couldn't talk anymore, there had been too much that had happened.

"Lets sleep." she whispered, again she was right on what we both needed. We entered the dark room, where Tara slumbered; I lay down beside my broken hearted sister, while Keara lay down beside me. Thoughts plagued my mind as I tried to sleep. Kofra had wanted me as her Alpha, but why? Daligulvens never looked outside of their own tribe for a pack mate. Maybe none of the other males had been strong enough, or could take her shit. What had happened to Black Mist? Why did he die, he was smart and a good fighter he should of ran from those stupid dragons . . . my mind finally drifted in too troubled sleep.

I awoke before the girls did and slipped out of the bed, they were still asleep, Tara, my sister, my friend, and Keara . . . my soul mate? It sounded weird even in my head, but I knew it was right in my heart. I exited the room and rummaged around in the kitchen and finally just ended up eating a box of cereal and finishing off the milk. I would buy some for Tara if she really wanted some, after my stomach stopped churning; I opted for a shower, letting the water get as hot as I could bare it. I stood underneath it, letting it slide down my body. Washing away the dirt, I grimaced at the bullet wound on my arm and the burn marks on my wrists, the bullet had luckily only grazed me, but the wound was black around the edges like a burn wound, both wounds would heal slowly. I sighed, and finished up in the steamy room, with a towel securely around my waist, I entered the room again,

JOURNEY THROUGH THE DARK WOODS

the girls were still sleeping, and quietly I got out clean clothes and changed in the living room. It felt good to be clean, to have the grime off of me. Tara would need a shower too, but I didn't dare wake her.

"Cody?" as though my very thoughts had waken her, she was standing in the hall way. "Shouldn't you still be sleeping?" I asked she shook her head, her rumpled curls falling around her face.

"Bad dreams, I need to talk about it, or its going to jump out of me." She whispered, as she made her way to the couch again, she sat and motioned me over, I sat down besides her. Putting a supportive arm around her, she sighed and snuggled against me.

"We had gotten separated, there were too many guards, and with Darrick taking care of the dragons, I had to get the guards off of his tail. I was a good distraction, but then something happened and all the guards fled. I figured you had killed Kofra and they had felt it. But then I felt Darrick, he was in so much pain, he didn't hide when the dragons got out of range of the castle, they had caught up with him. I ran to where he was, and it was almost too late, they had . . ." she paused, a sob escaping her lips, I told her she didn't have to continue but she pressed on. "I opened a portal right there, I pushed those damn dragons in too it, my energy was spent. I couldn't heal him Cody, I couldn't, I tried, but those stupid dragons had had too much magick on them . . . he died in my arms, that's when I felt the pain of it, and got your attention from it. Oh God Cody, what am I going to do? He was my only . . ." she stopped for the tears had started up again; I held her and hushed her like a small child.

"Its not your fault luv, he knew the risks, going in there so tired, he didn't even have any magick to truly teleport himself out of there. We should have waited, but it was the best time to attack before the full moon." The sobs quieted as she looked up at me, and nodded, without a word she pushed off of me and headed in too the bathroom, I heard the water running. Sighing, I stood up and went to the door.

"Want me to grab you some clean clothes?" I asked, I heard a faint yes, and headed back in too Keara's room. I wasn't a good judge of female clothing, so I woke Keara up, we had all slept for eight hours, and I figured she wouldn't hate me for it.

"The shower will make her feel better." Keara assured me as she dug through her clothes for something that would fit the taller girl better.

"Sadly, I don't think we're the same bra size, so a camisole will have to do." she whispered to herself, I almost laughed, they were about the same size of chest, but I wasn't going to point out the differences. After Tara emerged from the shower slightly better looking, she decided that she needed to head out for a little bit.

"There are a couple of things I must do." That's all she told us, we tried to talk her in too staying but she didn't listen, she said she would find me in a week or so. After all of it, we both, Keara and I, knew, that we could finally start a semi normal life together.

EPILOGUE

WE HAD FOUND a nice house in America, actually in the same town I had been in Oregon, called Newberg, it had a large basement where we fortified a place for me to stay during the full moon. Keara continued being an Earth Guardian and we lived quite well off of her money, but I couldn't be a slacker. So I still did odd jobs for random people, giving me things to do while Keara was away on 'business'. Tara did return to us, and asked to live with us. Of course we didn't turn her away; she claimed the basement as her room. Her heart was still mending but she did seem in better spirits and being around us was helping her. We soon decided that if we were going to live with each other we might as well get married. Tara had to forge a fake social security card and ID for me, but we ended up going to a little church with Tara and we were married there. It was strange seeing my human name on a little piece of plastic with a picture of me on it. Tara told me to get used too it, because we would have to move around after every fifty years or so. I understood that, when you only age one year out of two hundred or so it would make people talk.

A decade and a half in too our married life, we discovered that Keara was pregnant, it was a joyous occasion, Tara was flabbergasted and told me how strange a father I would be, but at least I had Keara. There was only two things haunting our minds, the child would be half werewolf that was just going to happen, the gene for it was too dominant. But if the baby was a female she would be chosen to become an Earth Guardian when she reached sixteen or seventeen. We devised a plan, if the child was a girl, I would leave home when she was two, and return to the Darkwoods, Juniper never checked who was staying in the cursed place, so I could slip in. There I would stay and await my daughter for her to get there and then help her out of the place. Keara agreed but was saddened at the fact that I would leave for almost fifteen years, I told her she would have Tara, but she just stared at me like I had a hole in my head. Which sometimes I thought I did with the looks those girls would give me.

In the middle of Keara's pregnancy, it had leaked out in too the Earth Guardian council that I was the father. So after a lengthy trial I was forgiven for the crimes I had done. My name was clean, and as long as Keara was my care taker, no Earth Guardian of any continent could touch me unless I had lost my soul and started killing again. I found it a good agreement.

A couple of months later, we were in the delivery room, Keara gripped my hand, and was yelling and the heat from the lamps and the different smells were really playing hard on my senses. I almost wanted to faint, but then I heard the doctor say something and then there was crying from the small infant. They cleaned off the baby and handed it too the exhausted mother, she cried, and held the baby to her. I looked down at the small infant in her arms, so small so fragile, yet someday would be quite powerful. The baby was a girl, which Keara named Raven, I thought it was an odd choice, but Keara told me she had her reasons. I didn't argue I wasn't the one who pushed the baby out of me.

"That means, we're going through with the plan." I whispered it was the next day we were home, the small infant was in her cradle asleep.

Keara nodded, "But not for two years, then it goes through." she left to go down stairs, I stared down at the little girl, who had a head thick with light brown hair with red in it, I smiled, multicolored hair, just like her mother.

"I love you Raven." I whispered, and stayed in the room too watch the little miracle that lay before me.